the Villa

Maureen Burton-Bukhari

 **Friesenpress**

Suite 300 - 990 Fort St
Victoria, BC, Canada, V8V 3K2
www.friesenpress.com

Copyright © 2016 by Maureen Burton-Bukhari
First Edition — 2016

All rights reserved.

No part of this publication may be reproduced in any form, or by any means, electronic or mechanical, including photocopying, recording, or any information browsing, storage, or retrieval system, without permission in writing from the publisher.

The characters and places depicted in this book are fiction. All references to Greek Mythology are solely the interpretation of the author.

ISBN
978-1-4602-7902-1 (Hardcover)
978-1-4602-7903-8 (Paperback)
978-1-4602-7904-5 (eBook)

1. *Fiction, Fairy Tales, Folk Tales, Legends & Mythology*

Distributed to the trade by The Ingram Book Company

1

There is a small fishing village named Forgotten Cove nestled in a quiet bay. It looks exactly like the picture used for the tourism postcard of Chaleur Bay. Chaleur Bay is located on the Atlantic Ocean a little over seven hundred and fifty miles north and a little east from New York City. Forgotten Cove is home to steep cliffs on its northern shore. These cliffs sometimes create severe wind gusts causing the sea conditions to become quite treacherous. Toward the south-western shore, the bay is covered in beach grasses and sand dunes creating the perfect habitat for several varieties of sea birds to nest. While on her morning walk, Hannah noticed the small white flowers from a wild strawberry struggling to grow among the grasses. She thought to herself how she often felt out of place living in this cove just as the strawberry plant oddly appeared out of place on the sandy beach.

The small population of a little over two thousand people living in Forgotten Cove is mostly fishermen and their families. There are a lot of summer cottages and a few newer bed and breakfast inns in the area. The village documents itself as a settlement in the late seventeen hundreds, with the first settlers arriving to fish the waters off the coast of Chaleur Bay recorded back as far as the early sixteen hundreds. Descendents of those early settlers still live in the older part of Forgotten Cove where the land meets the rock cliffs on the northern shore. The newer area of Forgotten Cove stretches along a sandy beach for miles heading out to the Atlantic and farther south to more populated places such as New York City and Boston.

For the tourists that visit in the summer, the attraction of the area is the beauty of the cove. The high rock faced bluffs provide a home for the abundance of birds nesting there. Flowers are growing out of the cliff walls as if they were carefully planted. These cliff walls fall down perilously to provide secluded beaches with the warmest Atlantic water north of Virginia.

Hannah had lived a few blissful years in Forgotten Cove, married to whom she considered to be her soul mate. He was Jack Gallegar. Their happy life abruptly all came to an end a little over a year ago. Hannah was now a widow. Hannah almost proudly presented herself as an expression of the grieving widow personified. She wore black every day, stayed at home, alone, without the benefit of a friendly smile from close friends. She had not experienced one peaceful night since Jack died. Hannah spent her days going over the confused and terrible dreams recurring since the accident.

In several of her dreams, Hannah stares out to the sea as the huge waves come crashing inward spraying her and the others that stood waiting with her on the shore. In some dreams she was not on the shore with the people from Forgotten Cove. Hannah could see herself standing on the fishing boat. This dream was an alternate version of the dream but with the same outcome. She wasn't with the people standing on the shore but was on the sea; specifically she clung to the remnants of the boat, mesmerized by the hypnotic thundering motion of the waves. In her dreams, she would become increasingly aware of the wailing sound that pierced her being to the very soul of it. The people standing on the shore were screaming to her, words she could not understand. What was wrong with them? Why did they just stand there and watch her struggle on the boat? Why didn't they at least make an effort to come out to rescue her? Couldn't they see she was clinging to the nets for her life, all bound up in the splintered wood of the partially destroyed fishing boat. The storm seemed to come up so suddenly, pounding the water with such a rage that it created frothy white-capped waves, moving forward without mercy toward the otherwise peaceful bay.

HANNAH JERKED AWAKE, STARTLED AT yet another of the repetitive dreams. She felt as if she had just crashed back into her own life. Hannah immediately felt her body to see if she was soaked in sea water. Shaking off these strange feelings, Hannah wondered just how a person could be in two places at the same time - on the shore and on the sea - as she is in her dreams. Why did the confusing dreams keep recurring on so many nights? Hannah had felt such a great loss when Jack died. The intellectual side of her told her the confusion in these dreams made sense since she had been so traumatized by the event of her husband's death at sea. The dreams occurred two or three nights weekly over this past year. The dreams wore her down.

"I really need to get myself back in control and remember the good memories Jack and I had. I must try to enjoy the beginning of the summer." Hannah said these words out loud, hoping she would take it as an order or a mantra given to her by some wise person. Tears sprung quickly to her eyes as she realised how vulnerable she felt and just how tired of the dreams she was right now.

Yesterday Hannah quit her part time job at the tiny book store. Her only real friend, Ellie, owned the only book store in Forgotten Cove. Hannah had more than enough with Jack's insurance money and their savings to live very comfortably. It was a little over a year now since their family fishing boat went down that dreadful night in the freak thunderstorm. It had not been easy learning to live alone again - especially in this place.

It was now a total of five years since she had fallen hopelessly for Jack Gallegar. They married quietly on the beach and settled into Jacks existing fishing business in Forgotten Cove. The two newlyweds took up residence in his family home. It was a small Cape Cod style house, very typical for the location. The cedar shingles that covered the house from top to bottom had turned grey long ago with age. Wild flowers filled the natural garden inside the fence that surrounded the house.

Hannah was a native New Yorker on a holiday to Chaleur Bay. It was truly a beautiful day five years ago when Hannah had literally run into Jack. He was dragging a torn fishing net across the sand from his boat for mending. Hannah decided this would be something she would like to help him do. Ellie told her that Jack would be expecting her to pay him a visit to learn about local folklore. As Hannah run forward to help him drag the net, he spun around. The two were face to face and nose to nose. Hannah laughed at this encounter. Jack smiled and captured Hannah's heart forever. This is how she met and married Jack Gallegar. It changed her life profoundly. Her professional career went from prestigious psychiatric nurse in New York to village fishwife. The locals in Forgotten Cove were a bit standoffish with her when they met her. This was because of her being an educated city person, especially being from such a big city like New York City. Part of it was the fact that her career was the dream of most young girls living in these small coastal towns.

The people of this quiet village did not want to lose their children to careers in a city like New York. Even now the townsfolk were only lukewarm with her except, of course, Ellie who was a few years younger than Hannah.

Ellie, her one and only friend grew up in Montreal. Ellie's family had retired from the city in order to live in Forgotten Cove. Her family opened a bed and breakfast for the hundreds of tourists that spent time here on their vacation. Many tourists pass through the area surrounding Chaleur Bay during the summer months making the business very successful. Ellie was only fifteen when her family moved to Forgotten Cove. Being a bit of the tom-boy, she immediately became a good friend of Jack Gallegar. It was Ellie who introduced Hannah to Jack while Hannah had stayed at Ellie's family's bed and breakfast inn. Ellie told Hannah that she should go to the dock where Jack's fishing boat was docked to learn the history of the area. Ellie had arranged with Jack to give Hannah a tour of the fishing boat. That was the day Hannah had run into Jack. Jack had decided the very day he met Hannah that he would marry her and keep her from ever leaving the small village. Hannah fell fast for Jacks weathered soft smile and married him on the beach in Forgotten Cove with Ellie by her side. The wedding was her dreams come true for Hannah. Ellie helped Hannah to find a seamstress to make over Jack's mothers wedding dress. They sewed it with yards of netting and white tulle cascading down as fish nets from her shoulders. The three of them picked huge baskets of wild flowers from the bluffs and spread them over the beach where they had the local justice of the peace marry them. The whole village of Forgotten Cove attended the ceremony. Truly the people who lived in Forgotten Cove were simple fishermen who appreciated the simple wedding ceremony of one of their favourite sons. Their education was at sea as was their father's before them. It was the same hard life. Jack Gallegar was the son and grandson of a fisherman from Forgotten Cove. The marriage meant new life for the community with young families staying here to run the family fishing business. The people of Forgotten Cove wanted this to happen rather than the young couple to go off to find work in the city. It was a beautiful day with a beautiful promise for a hopeful future.

Hannah had loved her nursing career but she loved Jack more. She grew up as the unfortunate child of a drug addict mother who could have cared less what happened to her, good or bad. She had learned independence at a very young age. This is what brought her to Forgotten Cove. Hannah's independence gave her the curiosity she had for adventure in faraway places.

Hannah thought to herself of dear wonderful Ellie. Ellie had stayed in Forgotten Cove with her parents when they retired instead of going back to Montreal. She opened the small bookstore at the bed and breakfast inn. This provided lots of information for the tourists that come to Forgotten Cove every summer. Ellie had been Jack's best friend since she moved to Forgotten Cove as a fifteen year old.

"Well, I should be grateful at least for Ellie," Hannah thought aloud, "I will work a little harder on trying to stop with this tragic widow attitude." She thought it might be comforting to just sit on the seashore and read her book. "Maybe have a lazy nap on the beach," Hannah's thoughts were continuously spoken aloud as she half-dragged her blue lounge chair, her blue blanket and the blue book bag filled with a few healthy snacks along with her unfinished book, "Wuthering Heights". This was the fifth summer she lived in Forgotten Cove and the fifth time she was reading it.

The book was special to her. It was Jack's mother's book. Before his mother died, she would sit on the beach reading this book. Hannah had learned that Jack's mother performed this ritual every summer and now Hannah was carrying on with this tradition in exactly the same way his mother had. It sometimes felt to Hannah that she was keeping the memory of Jack and his mother alive by doing the same. This kept her from feeling so alone. It gave her a sense of belonging to Forgotten Cove.

Hannah chuckled to herself, "Hannah, do I see a pattern here?"

She sometimes felt love had abandoned her the same way it did for the tragic Catherine of the book. It gave her a kind of comfort in reading this book over again. Hannah felt akin to Catherine, felt as if she had even known her to have lived in this small cove. Hannah settled herself into the beach chair and into reading the book to the end again.

High above Hannah the siren stood alone in the same place she stood one year ago, atop the bluff. The siren was watching Hannah all the while she was reading her book. The siren remembered the night she stared down at the splintered boat, pieces of it washing towards the distant shoreline. Aglaope, the siren, had summoned the sea to rise to her song. The song was hypnotic. It could paralyze the mind of a human. Aglaope had promised a soul to Persephone. This place, Forgotten Cove, was the perfect location to find such a soul.

On that same night Aglaope came to claim a soul, she was sure she saw her mother on the splintered fishing boat trying to stop the destruction of it. How had her mother known where she was? Aglaope traveled far from her home in a north and west direction. She found this cove, this bay that looked very similar to her island of Anthemoessa. The small cove was surrounded by high cliffs of jagged rock similar to her island of flowers. The cliffs dropped down to the sea that was forever crashing against the rocks, dashing to bits anything in its pathway. What intrigued Aglaope about this cove when she arrived here last year was the woman she saw on the fishing boat several times. The woman was with the fisherman whose soul Aglaope claimed that night. This woman looked a lot like her own mother. A fine boned creature, pale skinned as if the sun had never touched her. Maybe it was the ash-brown colour of her hair falling in tangled waves down her back. Whatever it was, the woman really resembled her mother.

Aglaope's mother was an immortal and a daughter of Zeus. Her mother was Melpomene, the Muse of Tragedy. Given that fact alone should have made Aglaope's life simply a life of perfection. That could never be. A twist of fate banished Aglaope with her two sisters, Pisinoe and Thelxiepia forever to the island of Anthemoessa to become sirens of the sea. Her mother, Mel or Melpomene, could have tried harder to have her and her sisters released from this punishment given to them by her Aunt Demeter. Aglaope blamed her mother for all of this, her unhappy destiny as a siren of the sea.

Now it seemed that her mother had followed her again today from the island of flowers to this bay on the Atlantic. Aglaope considered why her mother was on the boat with the fisherman that night a year ago. Her mother was trying to distract the fisherman from her sirens piercing wail. Aglaope had been watching the shoreline in Forgotten Cove earlier today in the morning for awhile and saw a woman wandering the beach area again that she was sure was mother. Here. Why? Why now? That fisherman's boat went down over a year ago, so why would mother be here in Forgotten Cove today? Aglaope could feel rage rising inside of her.

One year ago Aglaope lost sight of her plan to harvest souls to use as bargaining tools to fill the emptiness deep inside of her. Instead, she gave in to the futile feeling of rage against her mother. The action Aglaope took against the woman named Hannah was not satisfactory as she hoped it would turn out. It was an action that resulted in the death of Hannah's husband that caused an overwhelming sadness in Hannah's life. Aglaope felt great disappointment when she realized her mother was trying to interfere. Her mother suffered the same sadness in her own life with great loss. Aglaope felt her mother didn't see her own daughter's feelings of being alone.

ONE YEAR AGO, AGLAOPE HAD not only controlled but directed her rage by creating the late afternoon storm. Aglaope sent her rage outward toward the sea. She used this rage against the fishing boat and people standing on the shore. These were the good folk of the town. She felt powerful as they watched her performance with the demolition of the helpless fishing boat. It gave her the attention she craved. Aglaope never had this kind of attention from her mother. Aglaope had taken control of the waves as well as control of the destiny of another.

Aglaope was a true siren of the sea. It was her sirens song that sent the waves to the boat, splintering the wood then crashing them inward to the shore. This was a cause for great fear in everyone standing on the shore. It was fear of the power of the sea. She needed this attention. Aglaope wanted the villagers to notice there was a greater force causing this storm, destroying the fishing boat. As always, Aglaope continued to feel isolated. It was because she was alone. Part of her wanted to watch the waves with the villagers, perhaps to feel a sense of sharing and being more like one of the people from a community somewhere, anywhere. Aglaope felt confusion rising again. It was much like the confusion Hannah had experienced that night.

It was that night in the confusion Aglaope had felt herself layer, intruding deeply into the white pain of the one person on the shore that this was all directed at, this woman named Hannah, the one who looked so similar to her mother.

Aglaope guessed that this may be what she was looking for, a kind of satisfaction and with this satisfaction came revenge on her mother. That Hannah woman must have been a relative or even the wife of the fisherman on the boat. Aglaope only cared about one thing the night she took down the boat and that was punishment for this lady who stood helpless on the shore. To Aglaope it was necessary to claim the soul that night. The fisherman's soul was perfect since it satisfied the need to punish her mother by punishing the woman who looked like her mother. Aglaope vented her rage this way to forget the sadness she felt from being isolated a lifetime from her own mother. Now Aglaope would barter this soul. This too was part of her plan.

2

The sun in a blaze of old glory was slowly immersing itself into the sea. Melpomene stared at the lone body asleep on the blue lounge chair with the dog-eared book opened on her lap. Hannah looked peaceful now. Mel remembered how Hannah appeared to her the night her husband's fishing boat went down in the storm. Hannah was dazed and confused. Mel's daughter Aglaope had intruded into Hannah's mind with such ferocity that it left bits of the sirens experience in Hannah's memory. Mel remembered seeing Aglaope high atop the bluff, posturing in such a rage the night she created the storm. Hannah still possessed bits of Aglaope's experience of the night. Melpomene knew this to be true because she had also layered into Hannah and knew exactly what was in Hannah's memory of the night her husband died. Hannah actually had memories of knowing what happened on the fishing boat the night Jack died. Mel felt her own rage rising toward her daughter Aglaope. She tried to calm herself and think carefully of what it was she needed to do.

"*What is it I can do to help you, Hannah?*" Mel sent this whispered thought on the tail of the gentle late afternoon breeze.

When Mel felt this unrest inside of her, the wind picked up and chased loose bits of sand and leaves across the deserted beach causing Hannah to stir in her dreamless sleep. Did she want to intrude right now, to layer even further into this humans mind? Mel felt as if she knew Hannah well. She had shared with Hannah the loss of her beloved husband. Mel was standing close to Jack on the boat as it went down. Mel was watching Hannah that night and still now, a year later, she visited Hannah again in her dreams. The night Jack died had forever changed Hannah. Mel felt Hannah's great loss of stamina but curbed her rapturous voice from escaping her in a mourning lament.

Mel began thinking of her own past life, a time long ago when she felt truly happy. The world in which she lived was going to be so glorious, so heavenly. Now life sometimes felt small and unlived. There were many dangers on this earth that were stealing time. The world had become smaller. People traveled everywhere leaving no sanctuary for the animals. To simply layer the mind and control the glorious wolves as Mel could do was becoming a danger to the wolf and to her too. People were overpopulating this world. *People seem to inhabit every empty space on this earth of ours*, Mel thought. *There is nowhere the wolves can be at peace, nowhere I can be at peace.* A human year had passed since the fishing boat went down. There was something new in Melpomene's life at last. Hannah had become her new focus. This person had sparked her interest in life on earth again.

"*I feel I know who this Hannah is and who she will become to me. She is perfect for me to have as a new friend. She is a loner, though not by choice, of course. I saw Jack crying out for her the night his boat was taken down in the storm. Jack looked toward me and thought I was Hannah for a moment and even thought at one point that I was*

Aglaope in his confusion. I feel guilt for this grievous incident caused by my wayward daughter. This should have never happened. It did happen but I will make Hannah whole again, I promise."

Melpomene continued to reason with herself aloud. "It is a truth when I sing; everyone becomes mesmerized by my beautiful voice. I do not have an evil song with destructive intentions in my heart as my daughter Aglaope has. I am not the siren. I do have great power but why not enough power to have stopped Aglaope taking down the fisherman and his boat that night? It was her wail that was heard by Jack, her wailing siren voice was louder than mine that night. This one fought to keep his life, but a wooden boat is never a match for the sea. I tried to help him; he thought I was trying to destroy him. It is Aglaope who is responsible. How do I approach Hannah with all of this?" Mel laughed a gentle laugh and thought sympathetically, "No one can concentrate when I sing very gently. It is rapture, so beautiful and so distracting. I could sing to Hannah. Yet when I tried distracting Jack to undo what Aglaope was doing to him, I failed. It was futile, too late. Jack could only hear her evil wail and not my gentle song."

"If I can mesmerize with my song, why shouldn't that have been enough for Jack that night? Why was Aglaope's wail heard above than my soothing voice? I will get an answer for this.

At least the layered intrusions are beginning to work on Hannah. She dreams of me, this Hannah, she feels my presence now. Soon it will be natural for my will to be in control of her will. I will teach her to trust me." Mel stared again at Hannah, asleep on the lounge chair. "*I promise you, Hannah, I will help you,*" Mel said silently.

Melpomene, the Muse, had powers. She could find an empty space in the mind and create a warping in the memory bed. Next using this talent, she would begin to weaken this warp gently, so it would be easy to intrude into the mind. This was called layering, to create the space for herself in her host's mind with these intrusions of hers. She did this by finding the weak and empty spaces where a strong memory should be. Mel intruded into these spaces layer by layer until she completely inhabited the willpower and the mind of the person or animal. Sometimes Mel layered but did not want to control the mind. Mel did this only to share a life, the life she didn't have.

Melpomene started layering as a young girl but did not try it out on humans when she was a child. At first it was just the animals, mainly the wolves. All of her eight sisters implored her to stop doing this, saying that it was reckless to use the wolves and she should only use small animals. Mel knew they would love to share her ease with this power and would not be surprised if a few of her sisters had already indulged in layering a human outside the family. Mel and her sisters had varying degrees of this talent with Melpomene having the strongest ability of the sisters to layer. She considered it a divine right by her heritage. *Mother and father said we all must learn this craft well.*

Her family lived an isolated life. It was because of this isolation Mel felt she didn't always have a real life so considered these layered lives – shared or borrowed for a while - as part of her existence. Mel knew the layering could stop or break up in a human if there was too much distraction on her part or on their part while she was intruding. This meant at times she had to use large volumes of layering her own will into others. Hannah was an easy layer since Jack was taken from her. That life event had weakened Hannah's mind significantly. Since his death she was alone most of the time and the opportunity for Mel to be part of her life in layers existed.

Typically, multiple times layering her host enhanced the detachment zone, the dense, permeable layer that provided the plane of weakness in the person or in the animal that Mel chose. To become a host like Hannah it was necessary to form an entry, a sill in their mind similar to a window sill. Hannah fit this criterion perfectly. She was not in control of any part of her life since Jack died. The sill where Mel sat was open wide for anyone or anything to enter. This sill would lead right into where Mel wanted to be. She not only wanted but needed to be in control of this mind right now in order to help Hannah. Mel wanted more than this from Hannah. Melpomene felt she had found a kindred spirit, a new friend. This Hannah had suffered great tragedy the same way Mel had suffered tragedy by someone else's hand.

Close by, Hannah startled awake, again, with the memory of another strange dream. It was terrifying. It was the faceless woman pointing a finger accusingly, directly at Hannah, this time she was standing on the beach the night Jack died. This time she was feeling overwhelmed and broke into sobs of sadness for the tragedy life had dealt her. Hannah felt so alone here and considered maybe it was time to move on. Hannah would make the final decision to move back to New York but Jack kept her here. She felt confused. Hannah knew she should let go but something she shared with Forgotten Cove made her feel a little less alone. If she only had enough courage just to get back to the city and her old life, her life may look brighter. Maybe she could just keep her house here as a summer place, then she could get a life, network and find a new or old circle of friends. Maybe, just maybe if she talked to Ellie, the only other person in Forgotten Cove who was not descendant of someone from here. Ellie would encourage her. Hannah looked around the deserted beach, hoping no one witnessed her breakdown. She gathered her belongings together with the book, all dog-eared and headed home, feeling a bit more hopeful. A woman sitting alone on the beach waved to her. Hannah waved back to this friendly person. She felt a familiarity with the woman. She felt she knew her, thinking possibly she had just seen her in Forgotten Cove before today, she was unsure. Hannah headed home. It was late afternoon. Hannah decided to skip her evening meal in order to try to sleep again.

JACK STOOD ON THE DECK of the fishing vessel with a terrified look on his face. *"Who are you, how did you get here?"*

Hannah was puzzled at how odd it was for him to say this, *"Jack it's me, let me help you."*

"Get away from me," he screamed, *"I don't know you."*

Hannah reached out to grasp at his hand and Jack stumbled, hitting his head on the anchor, opening a deep wound. Blood spurted from the gash, running into his eyes. He tried to get up, to get back control of the boat. The sea had become very choppy and Jack knew he had to head into shore right fast. She tried to help him. He pushed at her to get her away from him and he fell again.

"Jack, please let me help you."

His scream pierced the night. *"No..!"*

Hannah woke in a start, crying and shaking. It was her screaming this time that pierced the night.

"Oh Jack! Why did you leave me? Why did you die? Why can't I find a little peace?" She tasted the salty sea water running down her face. Hannah sobbed, "Oh my God! I am truly coming undone. I am losing my sanity. I have got to do something."

HOURS LATER HANNAH SIPPED THE last of her morning coffee trying to lighten up from last night's dream. She had called Ellie and they were meeting for lunch at the book store. She didn't quite know how to approach the subject but Hannah knew she had to get some help. Walking down to the book store in the later morning she felt the pull of the sea. She honestly felt as if Jack or someone else were calling her to the sea. Those thoughts could become very dangerous. Hannah quickly brushed them aside upon seeing Ellie standing outside the book store waiting for her.

"Let's have lunch out here on the deck", Ellie said, and after more than an hour of what Hannah felt was raving, Ellie laid her hand over Hannah's in a gesture to comfort her.

"You know, you must have read stories of the sirens of the sea – that's what your last dream sounded like. Maybe you sleepwalked down to the shore. That would explain the salt water. I am sure that empathy is the reason you feel that you know exactly what Jack went through the night he died, Hannah, you loved him so much."

"But Ellie, then why is it I am on the boat in my dream, at least part of me is on the boat and another part of me is watching it go down from shore as we all did that night while waiting for Jack to make it back to land." Hannah started sobbing again. "Ellie, do you really think that I am dreaming I am like a siren of the sea claiming its sailors?"

When Hannah said this to Ellie, she looked deeply hurt. Quickly Ellie said to her, "I'm sorry, I just want to help you lighten up, Hannah. I know it's been hard but I am sure you are having anxiety dreams. Go back to work, get a distraction and start going out somewhere again."

Hannah said "Here?"

"Well somewhere, anywhere, I would hate to see you leave Forgotten Cove but do something to move forward. Don't become like the widows here, watching the sea for the fishing boats to return knowing damn well they will never come back."

Hannah looked incredulously at Ellie. "Ellie, in my dreams I don't watch the sea for fishing boats, I watch the shore."

Ellie remembered the night of Jack's accident. Hannah was standing on the shore staring out toward the boat. Ellie tried talking to her several times to comfort her but Hannah stood as if she were in a trance with her mouth agape. It looked as if she were singing a silent song, pointing toward the boat, with a horrid look of satisfaction on her face. Hannah did not respond to Ellie or anyone else that night as she stared silently out to the sea.

THE SUMMER MOVED SLOWLY. DREAMS for the future would never change the past. Hannah knew she had to make the change in her life now. She allowed herself only an hour a day with her book and spent the rest of her hours going over possible places to apply for a job position and a new life. Hannah was determined to change the situation she had accepted this past year.

3

Midsummer, a few weeks later Hannah dried a tear that fell on the last page of her tattered book. It stained the pages of a book that ended the life of Catherine, leaving Heathcliffe alone in his madness on the moors. Again Heathcliffe was lost forever in want of Catherine's love when Catherine had died leaving him truly alone. He could see her ghost wandering the moors but knew he would join her only in death. Hannah knew this would happen. Hannah silently questioned herself. *"How many times do you have to read this book?"* Hannah read "Wuthering Heights" every summer since coming to Forgotten Cove and her Catherine never had a happy ending. The educated part of Hannah knew this was how the story was written and it would never change. Hannah had started her ritual reading the book when Jack would be gone for days on the sea, fishing. The book was given to Hannah when she protested to Jack who wanted to pass the book on to Ellie for a sale in her book store. Hannah argued that it was not just a book but a keepsake from his mother. Jack's mother had owned the book for many years. When his mother died, it was the only thing he had not immediately parted with from his mother's scant belongings. Hannah had come to love the story as much as Jack said his mother did. Jack told Hannah of how he would be playing at the beach as a child and sometimes would sneak up on his mother who would be sitting on the shore reading "Wuthering Heights". He would ask his mother why she would read something that made her so sad. Jack's mother gave him the same reason every time he would ask her. She hoped one day to read it and the heroine, Catherine, would marry Heathcliffe. Even as a child Jack laughed at this impossibility. As Jack grew older, he heard stories from the old folk of Forgotten Cove of the rugged fisherman who was his father, lost at sea when Jack was only days old. Jacks mother spent her days alone at the seashore with young Jack waiting, watching. Every summer she read, "Wuthering Heights' while Jack run along the shore with his kite or as he built huge sandcastles. The sad book and the empty life made Jack's mother cry for the life she could never have. Hannah went over this story told to her by Jack. It made the book very dear to her.

"*That makes me so miserable to cry for Catherine and Jack's mother,*" Hannah was thinking, "*so why not try to read something else?*" Hannah looked around to see if anyone saw her in this weepy state. She was finally beginning to tire of the routine of spending her time being just sad with nothing else to interest her. There was only one other person on the beach this late in the afternoon on this early August day. It was that same woman she saw wandering along the shore watching the bluffs every afternoon Hannah had come to read at the seashore. She seemed close in age to Hannah. Hannah never saw her sitting on a beach chair, instead she would be just slowly wandering along the shore, looking out to the sea and up toward the bluffs. Maybe she was an artist looking for a good angle to paint. The summer brought so many people to Forgotten Cove, each with a dream and a life of their own. Hannah remembered seeing this woman watching her too, every time she had come to the shore to read this summer. She had questioned Ellie earlier in the summer to see if the woman was resident at the bed and breakfast. Ellie told her she had never seen the person Hannah described within the Forgotten Cove tourist community. Maybe she was renting a summer house somewhere. Maybe she was one of the summer tourists that just wanted quiet time alone. Hannah waved to her. The woman stared back in her direction. Hannah decided it would be more pleasant to make a friend instead of burying herself in the sad tale of Catherine and Heathcliffe. She could not change the outcome of the book any more than change her loss of Jack. "*Move on, Hannah!*" she said, silently to herself. Hannah walked over to introduce herself. That tiny event was the end of the life of being alone Hannah had chosen for herself.

The next morning Hannah was chatting to Ellie, "Ellie, I have found a friend, she is a bit of a loner but she seems somehow like an old friend. I feel like I have known her forever. Her name is Mel, she is a summer tourist. She kind of reminds me of myself, same long, wavy hair, no makeup, you know - the natural look. I invited her to supper tonight. Please come too. Oh Ellie, this feels so good to make a new friend and get moving forward in my life again. We were talking of travel and how much we both love to travel. She has a house in Jeddah of all places, would you believe it? I hope she will invite me there one day."

"Whoa, slow down Hannah, I think this is great news. This reminds me of how chatty you were when you first arrived in Forgotten Cove. You act like you finally have something to look forward to in your life. You just enjoy the company this Mel person gives you this evening. I have a few things that need to be done. Call me tomorrow to tell me all about your dinner and Hannah, please just enjoy this evening."

"Thanks Ellie, I will." Hannah got off of the telephone and started to prepare dinner for her guest.

Hannah felt that she did learn an awful lot personally about Mel yesterday afternoon in the short introductory exchange of who they each were. She comes originally from Greece. Her name was Melpomene but everyone calls her Mel, Hannah was told. Mel told her that she was from one of the oldest families in the Mount Olympus area. She had three daughters who were grown up but she looked so young, Hannah thought. Mel had told her that she was an advocate to save the earth from the polluters and big business. Mel's whole family were "caretakers' or stewards of the earth. That's what she said, Mel's words. She seemed to know a lot about the tragic accident on the fishing boat that caused Jack's death last year. It might be that the locals are still talking about it and Mel heard it from them. Hannah felt that Mel was such a genuine type of a person. She had only just met her but desperately needed this caring friend. It was a wonderful distraction. Hannah spoke aloud, "I guess some friendships are meant to be."

MEL ARRIVED FOR DINNER LATER in the afternoon. The two of them sat down and exhausted the fish and summer salads Hannah served for dinner. They settled into comfortable armchairs each with a glass of wine. The conversation covered everything from world history to personal events leading up to Jack Gallegar's death. Hannah felt almost relieved to share her most private feelings with Mel. It felt like the healing process had finally begun. Hannah felt purged from the heavy burden she carried from the wild dreams. Mel did not appear to judge her or think that Hannah was crazy for her dreams being so overwhelmingly vivid. Mel shared with Hannah that she reminded her of her younger sister Thalia. This new friend was just what Hannah needed. It made Hannah feel excited about experiencing life again and most importantly, she really felt a sense of urgency in moving forward with her life, soon.

The two women shared many evening meals as the summer started to show the seasonal changes needed for winter. The earth was preparing itself to sleep. It would soon blanket itself with brightly coloured falling leaves until spring many months from now. The smell that comes from those coloured leaves, more beautiful in death than life, made a person eager to be alive. Hannah loved this part of the year in Forgotten Cove. The smell of all of the foliage in this stage of decay filled the cooled evening air with a promise of early snow coming very soon.

One evening Mel requested Hannah share a little about her life. "Tell me about yourself, Hannah."

"There is not a lot to tell you, Mel," began Hannah, "I have never shared my childhood with others for fear of being judged. I was raised by a single mother who was completely disconnected from family life. Instead of sharing her life with me, she shared it with a needle filled with heroin. She was never home."

Hannah paused for a moment, and then continued, "I pretty much spent my childhood immersed in any book I could get my hands on. This reading led to a scholarship in a good nursing school for me to get my degree. After that I traveled to see every place I felt that I missed seeing as a child."

It was close to the end of September when Mel made an offer to Hannah that made her laugh at first. Next Hannah's mind rejected the offer as Mel maybe not being quite right in her mind.

Mel told Hannah that she had been there on the boat with Jack the night he died. She told Hannah how she reached out her hand to try to save Jack from being thrown against the broken mast on the boat. Mel told Hannah how Jack had listened to the wailing sound and become hypnotized by a siren of the sea. Mel further told Hannah that she tried to intervene by singing a beautiful gentle song, more beautiful than the siren could ever sing. The siren, Aglaope, had Jack held in a trance with a strong hypnotic spell. Mel added that Jack didn't realize that she was trying save him from this spell. Jack became confused with the siren's song. He saw her on the boat knowing she could not have boarded while he was at sea. Jack was confused and he called her Hannah. Mel seemed to know every detail of what happened on the fishing boat. It also seemed that Mel even knew every detail of what Hannah had been dreaming over and over again, since Jack's death. How could Mel have guessed what Hannah had dreamed? Did this mean that the dreams Hannah was having were all true?

Not only was this information hard to accept but it was what Mel told her after this account of Jack's accident. Hannah stared at Mel in disbelief. Mel told Hannah that she knew Hannah's husband had died by Mel's own daughters' hand. Mel related to Hannah that her daughter Aglaope was the siren of the sea that killed Jack. Mel's family were immortal beings. This meant they did not die, like Jack did. This lady, this Melpomene talked through the night. Hannah was a little frightened to ask her to leave. What she was telling Hannah was not possible in the human world. This all meant that Mel's daughter Aglaope had been here too in Forgotten Cove the night of the storm. Mel told Hannah that only in the last few decades had her daughter started traveling so far from home to this area of the world and she was definitely in Forgotten Cove the night Jack died.

Hannah began to feel a real discomfort with this tale. Hannah wanted Mel to leave and almost wished she had never befriended her. Stories of sea sirens were myths that old fishwives talked of when they couldn't deal with losing their husbands in fishing accidents. Another thought entered Hannah's mind. If this story, what Mel was telling Hannah were true and Mel was compelling Hannah to believe these words to be true, it could be the answer her dreams. Part of Hannah wanted to believe Mel; she felt somehow it kept Jack alive. But wait, how could this explain why Hannah dreamed of what Mel and of what the siren had experienced that night?

This night would be so long. Mel talked non-stop to Hannah making the case for all she was saying to sound very convincing. She told Hannah how she entered her dreams by layering her mind, seeing the little piece of Hannah's soul where Jack was a memory. Melpomene told Hannah that her daughter Aglaope had also layered into Hannah so hard and fast the night of the accident that bits of Aglaope's own memory were left behind inside of Hannah's mind. Mel told her this was why she dreamed she was on the fishing boat with Jack. The rough layering was the reason why Hannah had retained fragments of Aglaope's memory of the night. She related to Hannah that they must now put Jacks soul to rest if Hannah were to ever be at peace. It would stop the dreams. Mel told Hannah because of the layering Hannah felt comfortable with her as a new friend. This was why she felt like she knew Mel so well. Mel had become a part of Hannah because of the layering. Hannah had become a part of Melpomene too in a sense because she was layered gently with bits of Mel's kinder personal memories overlapping into some of the more grotesque bits of memory left by Aglaope. Mel had achieved this long term layering into Hannah's mind by triggering memories of herself and inserting them into Hannah's life, memories Hannah did not know existed as of yet. Mel had become very familiar with the area on the sill to enter the layer she made in Hannah's mind. This was the familiar window sill where Mel sat and could enter at will.

Over a second morning coffee, Hannah, weary from sensory overload and lack of sleep looked at Mel questioningly. She felt as though she was looking at an extension of herself or a sister or someone similar to one of them. Hannah tried to digest the information that Mel shared with her in the talk that went on through the night.

"Mel… did you ever want to be human?"

"Hannah, I am human, at least as far as this world is concerned, I am human. I've had three children and raised them to adulthood." Mel related this tale to Hannah.

The daughters she bore were unlike her. They had become sirens of the sea. Mel tried to control them and teach them of the softer beauty of the earth but had failed with this too. The daughters were banished from their Achelous River home as a punishment for a playmate being kidnapped while they were straying far from the safety of their home with her. When her daughters were banished from their home Mel sadly returned to her parent's family home on Olympus to try to reconnect with the peace she felt there. This was necessary for her sanity. After trying for years to help her daughters cope when they were banished to the island of flowers, Mel finally turned her tragedy inward. At the time only Mel knew of the depth of this sadness. Soon the world came to see her as the figure of tragedy she was to become in her immortal life.

Only in the past year after seeing the devastation caused by her offspring at Forgotten Cove did she decide that she would convince her sister muses to return with her to modern life on earth and stop this madness. The sisters must now show sympathy for all those who need it living on earth. This is necessary to help appease mother earth for all the injustice suffered at the hands of humans.

"My daughters did not turn out to be what I wanted for them Hannah. It made me so unhappy. It was a true tragedy for me. I left my husband and home, went back to my family home in the mountains of Greece. I tried to be happy but my sisters had all moved on with their own lives. I do have parents, you know. Our family life has had its share of happiness but also its share of not so happy times. Hannah, I can offer at least some of this world, my world, to you. You are alone. I feel like I am in some part responsible for the death of your husband."

"No, Mel, I can't believe it is your doing, it was a tragic accident! How can you say you are responsible for a freak storm, no person can be in charge of the weather enough to control it."

"Listen Hannah, I am seeing that you are finding all of this a little hard to believe. It is a lot to take in. It must be hard for you to not run from me and what I am telling you. Really, I am assuming you will want to retrieve Jack's soul to bury with his body. I must prepare. I must go for awhile to search for Aglaope. In the time I am gone I will have my staff prepare my family villa in Jeddah for us. I will send you airline tickets to travel to JFK international airport in New York City. You can fly by Saudia Air to Jeddah. I will arrange to have you taken to the villa and meet you there. I have a world to share with you."

4

The nine children, all girls, born of Zeus and Mnemosyne are called the Muses. They were born in Pieria. Mnemosyne was their mother; a beautiful immortal titan woman whose given domain by birth-rite was to rule was over the hills in Eleutherae. People living down at the bottom of Mount Olympus heard stories of the muse's mother, Mnemosyne. The stories were of a true goddess guarding the gates to the underworld. Zeus was their father. He was the immortal god of Olympus. He fathered the nine girls with Mnemosyne. At the end of each of her nine month pregnancies, Mnemosyne bore him a beautiful daughter. All of them were blessed with an unearthly beauty. The girls shared with their mother one mind filled with the memories of the great empathetic love she had for this earth. The muses were free spirits who would learn to bare their souls to everyone in song. They would give their hearts to the earth and to Mount Olympus. They were born in a cavern which was their family home a little way from the top of snowy Mount Olympus in a remote unknown area. It was an isolated life and so the girls socialized with each other, the animals and the birds as their closest companions. The family, friends and relatives were the people from whom they became educated, in song. Hermes, Apollo and Perseus were closest to them in their early years. The muse sisters learned to look to the heavens for guidance for their beautiful and rapturous words. Music was given to them to learn by their parents as a craft to take them through life. The sisters looked to Mother Earth for inspiration in this guidance. Aside from family, the neighbour living closest, in another cavernous abode higher up on Olympus were Ceto and Phorcys. They had three daughters who roamed the mountain peaks with the nine muses. Ceto and Phorcys had several other children. These other children kept their distance from the muses.

ON A LAZY LATE AFTERNOON Melpomene, as a small child often roaming the mountain meadows had an encounter with the wolf who would become her companion. It stopped her in her tracks - she knew instinctively to remain still. The sleek grey wolf blinked and tilted his head as if to ask who or what she was. The child took this as a sign that he was not going to attack her. They sat together in the wild grasses. Mel had learned to layer and to read an animal's body language while trekking the high mountain meadows with both her siblings and with adults. Mel thought to soothe this wolf today by singing pretty sounds to him. At her tender young age her voice was very developed. Mother told her that she had an angelic voice that would soothe the savage beasts. Someday the world would come to hear of her mournful yet beautiful song. As she breathed out effortlessly a rapturous sound filled the late afternoon quiet. Mel knew that even the birds would silence their song to hear her lament. The sounds penetrated the forest to the top of the tree line where many caverns opened into private dwellings. She thought of her mother, waiting for her in one of these cavernous homes. Mother may even hear her song today. Her family lived deep in a fortress close to the top of Mount Olympus. This was a safe haven for the children of Mnemosyne and Zeus. This is where the muse sisters practised the crafts they had learned from the immortals.

The wolf lay down at Mel's feet blinking away memories of a greater freedom once enjoyed on Mount Olympus, a freedom from being tracked and hunted by the fearful people who lived down the great mountain. It seemed that all life on the Gods earth seemed to be still at this moment, listening, along with this magnificent grey male. They were listening to Melponeme sing. It was as if the earth itself were mesmerized by her voice. Mother Earth needs to hear my song of rapture she thought as she moved her fingers slowly in the warm silken hair of the wolf's nape. The contentment Melpomene felt that day would not last forever except in her memory. Mel had been given this exact memory from her mother and her love of Olympus from her father.

Melpomene was different. She knew she was not the same as the children from the villages below the high peaks but she was also considered favoured by the immortals. This was due to her angelic gift of song. Mel and her sisters all possessed powers, gifts given by the immortals. Zeus was their father and Mnemosyne, their mother. This made the nine girls different from all other children of immortals. This gave great opportunity that all others could never hope to have. Their parents instructed the girls, all nine of them to guard their self wisely from other humans. One day they would come to understand how to use their gifts of song and words that were bestowed upon them from the heavens by birthright. Mother told Mel that her voice would come to enrapture others, capturing the very heart of their soul, no matter how good or evil that soul may be.

Melponeme would learn in her childhood that the world would come to question the union of her parents. She was already aware at a young age that father had many other families. Maybe she would meet the other siblings one day.

Close to the top of Mount Olympus the forests began thinning into open meadows. Abundance was a way of life for the inhabitants of the area. A lot of the flora and fauna were unique to that specific area. The soft meadow where Mel and the wolf lazed was fragrant with dazzling wildflowers. As the wolf slept at Melponeme's feet she gently stroked him. A deep rooted feeling of sadness began to awaken inside of her that day, overwhelming her. She blinked away a tear in her eyes and stared with question to the heavens.

Even at this age Melponeme was puzzled at these gifts her father told her were good gifts to be used for the benefit of others. She felt a little uneasy with the thought of what would happen if an animal didn't enjoy her song and didn't want to listen to her. A continuing inner sadness gave way to a feeling of being very alone. This feeling of being alone gave way to a momentary darkness that resided somewhere deep within her soul. Mel realized that she would someday sing so sadly it would pierce the heart of those who would hear it similar to a sharpened dagger piercing the soul. She blinked the tear that slowly made its way to her lips. Mel touched the salty liquid. These thoughts quickly fled. For now, Mel would enjoy her childhood and the silky coat of the sleeping wolf. She would someday roam the earth cautiously on high alert like the wolf - but not today.

Today Mel would find her friends Stheno and Medusa, two of her three friends who lived close to their cavern. The girls spent the years of knowing each other chatting about how one day they would all be mothers and raise their daughters on Olympus, the same way they were raised by their parents. Medusa was the eldest of the three friends. She was angelic and caught the attention of every male child on the mountain. The words were soft spoken from her lips. It was said by the immortals that Medusa could be an angel if they were personified on earth. When the sunlight touched Medusa a golden aura haloed her body. The girls all knew even in their childhood that Medusa would find a husband sooner than of all of them since she was so naturally beautiful.

As the years passed Mel and her sisters matured and grew closer. They became more as friends as much as being sisters. This was partially because of the isolation on Olympus that it was necessary to be companions as well as being siblings. Melpomene felt as close to Stheno, Euryale and Medusa, the daughters of their closest neighbours, as she did to her sisters. The girls matured all sharing their secret desires with each other of impending marriages. Melpomene felt very close to Thalia and Calliope, her two favourite sisters. Calli was older, she was the wise one and Thalia was younger, the fun one. Calli would entertain the impressionable Mel and her friends with ballads of faraway lands. Calliope traveled a lot with father. Calli became one of his favourites. Sometimes Calli would talk for days on end trying to impress Mel with very convincing versions of how father would let her mediate differences of opinions in the younger immortals. Calli confided to Melpomene that father had brought Hermes with them often and Hermes was obviously let do as he pleased. Zeus had a special place in his heart for Hermes. Hermes was his son. He was born of Zeus but not of Mnemosyne. Zeus had bestowed the gift of winged sandals to Hermes for swift travel. This meant Hermes was a favoured child since Zeus was careful not to show favour with his children by giving them gifts of such a treasure. Hermes became very close to Calliope throughout those years, as close as any brother would be.

Thalia was younger than Melpomene. She always had a smile on her face and a soft laugh to follow it. Thalia would entertain anyone who would listen with humorous stories from the homeland peaks. She found almost any incident on Olympus to have a lighter side. Often when Melpomene would be trekking high in the mountains she would hear the laughter of Thalia and Apollo. Apollo too, was a friend and a cousin. He loved Thalia as much as he loved visiting the beloved home of Zeus on Olympus.

The sisters learned through the years to fine tune their unique gifts. They possessed song, the spoken word, great grace and beauty. Each of them possessed a gift to make them a little different from the other. These gifts became a power for each of them, a power that they used only when needed. The Muse sisters would later learn to use their powers to get what they wanted and what they needed in their lives. The sisters shared the great natural beauty of their mother, Mnemosyne. It was a gift Zeus gave all of his children. Zeus gave his children beauty, strength and power.

Another of the inherited powers passed from Zeus to the muses was the power to layer. This power was a dominant power in some of his children and in a few of the others it was not as dominant. This meant they were less of an adept at the layering so would work hard to perfect it.

By using the power of layering a person could intrude into the empty spaces and openings in the human spirit or the soul, entering into their mind and taking over their willpower without the person being aware. Some wanted to say it was like possession but the user did not possess the spirit completely. The user invaded small areas of the soul in layers and resided only for short stays. Only the true immortals had the power to layer and draw strength into themselves by these intrusions. The daughters of Zeus drew strength from this craft as they became more of a seasoned practitioner. They were born of immortal parents. Layering gave them the understanding to slow themselves into the human world and live amongst the humans. The muses used this power to spend time on earth in the plane of human existence. They also learned to enhance their power to walk in the ethereal plane. It was by practising this power using layering to rise above time. Without time slowing them they could travel to another location in an instant. Immortals and those born of immortals could choose time periods of the earth since they were never bound by time. They would sometimes choose a situation that drew their interest such as plagues to be of assistance to humans. Mel came to love the great old cities of the world built on the seashores. She found the areas that experienced the most tragedies drew her interest. Her curiosity about deep inner sadness and human behaviour in a tragedy would sometimes cause her problems. Mel felt that she was born to endure great sadness. It was to become part of her life.

Mel understood the craft of layering and the great amount of energy it gave them. Energy taken from the soul of the other living entity was not felt by a host. At first Mel only layered into animals. The wolf that lay at her feet as a child listening to her rapturous song became a steady and willing participant. If Mel could love unconditionally the way a human loved a pet, then this would be the animal she loved. Children were always willing participants in layering. Their innocent nature sensed that she and not any one of the immortals would ever hurt them. Some adult humans knew of them and always older humans close to death would welcome her. They knew they would soon join her world, not as an immortal but as a member of our great cosmos.

Like an open window, the Muse would sit on the window sill and wait until the window would open further to enter. Sometimes the host entity felt something they could not explain such as an empty headed feeling, sadness or an extreme tired feeling. Humans sometimes would occasionally say they felt like someone just walked over their grave. This was the feeling when an open window was being entered. When a Muse returned to the same layered entity a second time it would be easier since they knew exactly where to go. Through the years the Muses learned not to use the same human for great lengths of time. It was to prevent the Muses befriending someone they layered into. This was because they were immortals not meant for the human world. They were taught to be gentle while on the sill, since forcing their way roughly into a layer would leave bits of their own memory embedded inside of the person or an animal.

5

It was in the early years of her life and learning, a great tragedy occurred on Olympus that would come to end Mel's innocence. The tragedy began the overwhelming sadness that defined Melpomene as the Muse of Tragedy. The sadness began stealing into the fabric of Mel's being. Poseidon, who was her father's own brother, lured her friend Medusa to a temple one afternoon. Poseidon raped her friend Medusa. After this event occurred, Poseidon's' mate Athena wanted revenge on Medusa. Athena cast a vicious spell on Medusa that stripped away her angelic beauty and gave Medusa a hideous head covered in writhing snakes. Whispered conversations said a person would die if they looked upon Medusas face. Father told the girls they would never see their childhood friend Medusa again. Medusa and two of her sisters would be banished forever to an island named for them. It was referred to as the island of the Gorgons. The once close relationship between the house of Mnemosyne and Zeus with the house of Ceto and Phorcys was forever damaged. It could never recover after the death of the innocent daughter of Ceto due to the decisions Zeus made after the incident. Through the millennia the two families remained as neighbors but the path to one another's door had long since grown over with wild raspberry bushes. Mel mourned Medusa as she would mourn a death, alone, atop Olympus with the wolf at her side. Her song was so sad in those days, it made the leaves on the trees droop, heavy with tears. The immortals and half mortals began at this time to whisper of the tragic aura beginning to envelope Melpomene.

Through the centuries Melpomene busied herself, becoming intrigued with what humans did to this earth. Mother Earth had seen and been through some very sad situations. Humans had been ruthless and uncaring about the state of the earth. Melpomene convinced the Muses to decide that they should now make a commitment to earth. It was now time to give help to Mothers Earth's environment and warn people of just how devastated Mother Earth felt. Mother Earth seemed to be retaliating with floods and earthquakes but these disasters were only a beginning of larger disasters to come. The muses would seek to try to restore harmony and calm to the earth, their beautiful playground. Soon they would all return to Mount Olympus to decide how this could be done. This would become their life's work. But first Melpomene felt she must make the situation her daughter Aglaope had brought upon this human named Hannah come to an end. Mel knew this would do little to defuse the immortals growing anger against her daughter for the reckless life she was living. Melpomene sometimes felt overwhelmed with this most personal tragic event seeming to spiral out of control even further from any resolution. This happened when Aglaope decided to leave Anthemoessa to search for souls for Persephone. Aglaope believed that somehow she would be forgiven for something that happened so many centuries earlier when she was a child, something that she should never have been made responsible for happening. Mel thought back to the days when she was a child and life was a little easier.

Year earlier as the sun rested, feeling quite heavy, over the Red Sea, the world was indeed a very different place. The sun was huge, orange and still on fire. It was as if dusk would never come. The mournful call to prayer for the dutiful filled the empty landscape. Mel startled awake. Sunset and fog or was this a dreaded sandstorm surrounding the city. The air was not clear. Their father had taken all nine girls to Jeddah. The heat had been very oppressive during the day so Melpomene and her sisters could not enjoy the day at the seaside. She would ask father if she, Calliope and maybe Thalia could walk to the market in "old town'. The whole city was old but her father always called the market area "old town' instead of Jeddah or the market. Zeus had entertained his daughters during the afternoon with the story of the grave in old town. The local people said the first woman was buried in old town. The first woman had traveled many hundreds of miles to meet her husband. The return journey was not to come about for her. She died there and was laid to rest in a grave near the sea. The grave was not marked by a monument. It was a grave, a place of reverence, a place where the first woman's remains lay. The future generations of the earth would all come to know some day that this spot marked the grave of the woman called Eve. This was one of the few reasons their father loved the city. It was old and the stories that surrounded it were old. Jeddah was evolving but always honored the past. The cement that built the city was made from sand, clay and seashells from the Red Sea. The villas were built in such a way to maximize the air flow through the buildings. Cool night air became trapped inside of the buildings. The decorative latticed windows were then shuttered during the day to avoid the sun, keeping the inside tolerable.

The summer was too hot mid-day to be outside but in the evenings when the sun dropped from sight the city was wonderful.

Mel and Thalia sat on large satin floor cushions in the sitting room with father.

"Papa," Mel began, "Calliope, Thalia and I want to walk to the market this evening, can we, please?"

"I will leave soon to check on our villa's progress, I want to have it prepared for your mother when she arrives next week so please stay here this evening."

Mel knew not to argue with her father so decided to wait awhile for Papa to leave. She then begged Calli and Thalia to come with her to the market.

"Mel you heard Papa, the sun has set and it is so foggy, so please do as you're asked. Stay here with us". That was the final answer from Calliope, the level headed sister who happened to be in charge right now.

Mel ignored this and slowly edged out of the second floor sitting room. She quietly descended the stairs and opened the door into the evening fog. The smell of the air was hot, sandy and wet. The warmed breeze was almost non-existent but still carried the perfumed smell of Oudh. Jeddah was very humid. The wetness clung to your clothing and run off your body in a million tiny rivulets within seconds of going outside. Mel saw several camels nearby, their owners standing close by to them, talking in a very animated way. They were wearing covers on their faces and heads to protect them from the fierce heat. Melpomene looked around from the high step where she stood and noticed a large travel trunk with brightly colourful cloth hanging out from it. She couldn't stop herself. Mel ran over to see the beautiful silk fabric. When she drew close to the half opened trunk she could smell the warm smell of Oudh, the perfumed wood that was buried sometimes in the hot sands of the desert to release even more oil than the water distillation gave to it. Oudh, the woody substance was to be used as perfumed incense to burn in ornate burners. Mel started to raise the lid further on the trunk to see more silks when her hand touched something that felt sticky and wet. In the semi-darkness she could see that it was blood. This frightened Mel. She turned and ran back up to the safety of the second floor sitting room, frightened that the men in the area may see her at the trunk. She placed her head on a cushion to wait for Papa and dosed, awakening when she heard father return much later. Mel knew she had to risk the wrath of her father.

"Father, I went out, just to breathe some night air and I saw a travel trunk. I opened it to see the beautiful silk fabrics and there was blood on them. I am so frightened that someone hurt a small animal," Mel sobbed into the safe arms of her father. "Please, can we see why this has happened?"

Zeus scooped up his daughter and asked her to show him where she saw this trunk. Down into the street they went and over to the trunk. Zeus put her down to the ground and opened the trunk. Inside the trunk were all of the colourful hand spun silks from the orient, as beautiful as one would ever imagine. There were containers of Oudh ready to be sold in the market. Something moved inside the trunk. Zeus pushed the silks aside. There was a young girl hiding among the layers of fabric. She appeared frightened of what they would do to her. The girl was close to Melpomene's age. She was bleeding from a small gash on her head. Zeus gathered her up and they carried her up the stairs to the upper floors of the temporary residence.

Zeus questioned the small girl and found she was taken from her home high in the orient's mountains known as the Himalayas. Her father was a poor goat herder in need of feeding his family so he sold his daughter to a rich man to use as he wished. The tiny girl could not work hard enough for this family so they hit her in the head, hoping it would kill her. Next she was put in the trunk to die. Zeus soothed the girl. He gently tended to the gash in her head.

His anger at those who did this to her could not be disguised. "Children are to be cherished not sold as property. You will have a house to live in with a family. Our family villa is ready tomorrow. It will be your home with us whenever we are here in Jeddah. We will send for your family and our villa will always be your family home while we are in Jeddah and even when we are not here. What is your name, girl?"

The girl smiled cautiously for the first time and meekly offered, "I am Hayghar."

Years later Melpomene stared at the beautiful villa walls, grown over with wild ivy many years ago. The walls protected the family that would live here forever. The memory of her father's unconditional kindness toward Hayghar that night made her a little sad, missing those who are no longer of this earth except in spirit. The villa has stood for hundreds of years. Yes, there have been updates. Jeddah was now a modern glass and steel metropolis that surrounded the old town and the grave of the first woman. Hayghar has been buried as was the first woman without a monument to her life, gone now for many years. Hayghar's memories along with old town Jeddah still exist today inside Melpomene as the bride of the Red Sea. Hayghar's children and grandchildren have been caretakers of this villa for generations. This would continue to go on as long as there were descendants of Hayghar who would want to share their life with the muses, their parents and their offspring.

Mel thought fondly of Hayghar. Her descendent Arabella was now the person in charge of the villa. Mel saw much of Hayghar's spirit in this young woman. Hayghar was probably only twelve earth years in age when father pulled her out of the trunk. Hayghar had worked hard for them at the villa. She showed pride in her new home and served the family faithfully, teaching her offspring the necessity to please the family of Zeus. Achelous and Melpomene also brought their offspring to Jeddah just as Zeus and Mnemosyne had done. Hayghar's descendents tended the daughters of Mel and treated them as their own. Those days were long ago and are now gone except in fond memory. Mel was here to inform Arabella of the guest who would be arriving. She further instructed Arabella that the guest was a simple human not an immortal or even a half mortal. The house would be open to the guest as if she were in her own home.

6

The Saudia Airlines flight seemed to float through the air. It felt as if it was held up by a puppet master, directing it's every move. The sky was cloudless; the sand below was only a slight shade off of the colour of a pure white cloud. The sea color was a true aqua. Hannah could to see into the sea right down to its coral reefs. This is the Red Sea. The plane banked suddenly. Hannah gasped as a city unlike any other she had ever seen came into view. The buildings were so modern and huge. Jeddah looked untouched by man. Even at this descending height, Hannah could see the obvious absence of people. A calm, disembodied voice spoke through the cabin in Arabic as the man sitting next to her closed his eyes and began to recite what seemed to be a prayer. This startled Hannah. She thought to herself the man she had carried on a great conversation with throughout the flight was praying because the voice said they were going to crash land. Hannah became agitated. The man sitting next to her finished praying, then said to her, "We have arrived in Jeddah."

"Excuse me," Hannah said, "I thought for a minute we were going to crash because you started praying."

He laughed quietly, spoke very softly and told her he was happy to be back in his country after his visit to a Washington hospital. He told her that he was giving thanks for this safe arrival. They chatted politely for awhile and then he left his seat, leaving Hannah behind to breathe in her introductory scent of Saudi Arabia, the smell of Oudh. The plane seemed to circle the city endlessly until the sky became lavender with a million silver nightlights. Hannah felt a peaceful feeling descend upon her, a rare feeling for her since Jack had died.

Hannah was told by Mel that she would be greeted by someone who would aid her in navigating her way through the airports infamous red tape. People, especially women, were not to be alone and unless you were greeted by someone, you may sit for hours until the airport personnel decide your fate. It took her more than an hour just to get outside to the limousine that would take her up into the palace area of Jeddah, overlooking the yacht filled harbor. The heat was oppressive. She was wet from the humidity and it was past the end of September. Hannah wondered how anyone could survive this city during the summer.

The sleek limousine entered through a pair of huge iron gates, proceeded down a long drive to an area that looked like a replica of ancient Greece. Statues of the ancient gods filled the gardens which were everywhere in sight. There were fountains towering above the foliage in every corner of the courtyard with smaller fountains on both sides of the drive extending down the length of the drive to the main house. Orchids of every color filled the well-tended gardens. Jasmine filled the air and wisteria vines cascaded down the walls of what seemed to be the main house just because of the size. The scent of Saudi Arabia overwhelmed Hannah. It was definitely the largest house she would enter, more of a palace than a house. Hannah was met at the entrance of the house and escorted inside by a young woman named Arabella. She was of few words when she introduced herself. Arabella led Hannah through marble floored corridors to a wide ornate marble staircase. Hannah was taken upstairs and led down to the end of one wing of the mansion into to a bedroom suite as luxurious as any palace she could imagine.

Arabella spoke briefly to Hannah, "You should calm yourself and collect your thoughts. Will you be in such an awe-struck state when you will be in the presence of the goddess? Melpomene will be generous to accommodate you with your needs. Accept her gift to put your husband's soul to rest so he will be at peace. The gifts from the gods are not to be rejected. You will feel the goddess sharing her thoughts and talking to you with a gracious smile. Respond to her in the same manner. Nothing will harm you in her presence."

Hannah asked quizzically, "Are you talking of Mel?"

Hannah felt numb. The lady she met in Forgotten Cove was indeed a real goddess, an immortal. Hannah was feeling the far reaching impact of the direction her life was taking on. What Arabella said to her was not something she felt she could understand while she felt so tired, so overwhelmed with everything that happened in the last few months. She wanted to take a soothing shower. Did Hannah want to taste the fruit that filled many bowls or just to smell the jasmine that filled every corner of the room? She opted to give in to the worst jetlag she had ever experienced in her life. With her mind racing, Hannah lay on the soft bed remembering Arabella told her there would be an offer to put Jack's soul to rest. Hannah slept the sleep of the dead for hours without dreaming.

When Hannah awoke it was to the sound of a call to prayer. She opened the window to a terrace filled with potted date palms. A blast of heat that could only be compared to opening a very hot oven assailed her. It soon mixed with the frigid air coming from air conditioners in her rooms. She looked to her left and right to take in the massive building where she would be housed for the next month. The sky was deep lavender with more stars than she ever remembered seeing in her life. Hannah took in the view of the harbor and the lights from the huge city before leaving to see the rest of the villa

The house was indeed a palace. There were so many rooms, all with a private terrace. From her own heavily draped windows Hannah gazed further around the area, taking in the miniature rain forest below. Hannah felt she had never seen such a lush tropical garden aside from a botanical garden at the zoo. New scents filled the air with jasmine growing inside and outside of the house. The rooms also smelled of makalat oil which was known to man as perfume of the gods. The servant that accompanied Arabella expressed this to her earlier when Hannah questioned the smell in the bedding and towels. Smoke spiralled as it rose from the Oudh or the agar wood as it was more commonly called. In the corridors Oudh filled the many incense burners placed throughout the house and now it filled her senses.

Hannah was taught all about Oudh from the native of Jeddah, the man she sat beside on her flight. It turned out that he was a local doctor on the same flight to Jeddah. He told her about the practice of using Oudh as a perfume.

Some trees growing in the far eastern jungles of Indonesia, specifically an evergreen tree would sometimes be attacked by fungus-carrying insects that bore into their trunk. It is similar to the same thing happening to us when we become infected by a bite from an insect. Our body's immune system produces a fighter called white blood cells to combat the infection. In the tree the same response is set into action. It will start producing a fighter substance to combat the infection. This fighter substance is seen later as a scar on the tree. On a person it appears as pus that scabs over the skin.

Over time, sometimes years, the infection grows and so does the scar from the infection. The scar is called agar wood and is a natural aromatic. It is harvested and distilled through water for months. The product of the distillation becomes an aromatic perfume or incense sold for enjoyment. The human senses feel pacified and stimulated from this scent. Hannah was feeling this as she thought of the conversation with the very polite doctor on her flight to Jeddah.

Hannah began to feel almost giddy with so many new experiences since boarding the plane at New York's JFK airport for her flight to Jeddah. She prepared herself to be ready for the day as she watched the lavender sky fade into the red and gold sunrise. Hannah was taken to a beautiful reception room for morning tea with Melpomene. The servant Arabella who met her at the entrance had been in the house for generations along with members of her family. The house staff were all descendants of Hayghar, the girl Mel found when they were both a child. Hannah had learned of this from Mel the night Mel filled her mind with stories of her own life. As promised after wonderful tea from the orient's finest collection, Melpomene sat down with her to relate to Hannah how her sisters also spend time in the villa in Jeddah. Mel talked further of how Hayghar's family had come to be a trusted part of their family. Melpomene waited each time as Hannah digested what she was telling her and would then relate more of her story.

"When my father sent me to marry Achelous, I went to his home with my sisters and mother as escorts. I was very young. Until that time I had lived with my sisters as my only real companions high up in the Olympus peaks. I was so very happy there. The only fiends I ever had that were male were Perseus, Apollo and Hermes, who were also related as half-brothers and cousins."

Hannah nodded. Mel continued, "Getting married to Achelous was most frightening for me. My sisters and I had learned of the ways we could manipulate nature and create magic in those peaks. We learned to layer and to teach earth creatures such as the wolves how to communicate their feelings to us. We learned to travel quickly without being seen but only went the short distance down the mountain. I had not learned of sharing a life with a stranger such as the one I was about to marry. We rarely left our home without other family members on Olympus. Zeus was a stern father and Mnemosyne was a careful mother. Mother knew that the immortals of the underworld were always looking for a mate. They would steal children for mates and we were nine young girls.

I was wed to my husband Achelous who loved the river more than me. He was god of the Achelous River, a powerful wealthy man and so for this reason I was sent to live with him, to be his wife. Although I was a little fearful of him, I did learn to care for him. We were happy for the first while. I bore him three daughters, three beautiful daughters. I taught them the ways of layering. I taught them how to sing into the wind to please all life on this earth. My daughters inherited my voice. They played with the sounds to make even more rapturous melodies than I had learned to make. The girls rivaled me at every moment as they grew. Achelous, their father was an aggressor, unafraid of anything and so my daughters inherited this aggression and the wanderlust from him. I seemed to be always out in the meadows looking for where they had run off to explore. Sometimes they would wander far from home and I was afraid for them. I missed the safe haven my family had provided on Olympus. I felt sometimes that I was failing my family in not providing safety on the river. Sometimes I longed to have my mother and sisters closer. Sometimes they would come to visit and even spend years with me. When my family come for long periods of time my daughters would even challenge their gifts and their song. My daughter Aglaope, whose appearance is the most similar to mine, was the most challenging for me. She was defiant like her father. Aglaope tried to best her aunts in song and in beautiful words. This was a little reminiscent for me of my mother telling me as a child that I would be known for my rapturous song more than any other of her children. It caused me to be very competitive when singing as it did for her too.

One summer when the girls were just past puberty, we had guests. Father's sister, Demeter and her daughter Persephone decided to stay on the river awhile. Persephone wanted to be around other children close to her age to share the secrets that young girls share with someone other than their mother. Demeter is my aunt, my father's sister and so Persephone is my cousin even though she was of my children's age group. Persephone was everything that my daughters were not. She was happy, always laughing and very demure. She never challenged her elders. Persephone was a delight and the centre of Demeter's world.

The children were at play one afternoon in the meadow and Persephone was viciously abducted. My girls had taken her far from the safety of our home to run free in the fields. The girls described Haides to us as the abductor. Demeter blamed my children for this and doomed them to search the underworld for Persephone. My daughters would be doomed to sing a song that would cause a fatal lethargy in humans but would not have the same effect on the immortals. She gave each of them wings and later on, the ability to change from the wings to a half fish body so they could search the sea for Persephone. The girls begged their father Achelous and me to stop Demeter's madness. We tried. We begged Demeter. Instead, in her anger, Demeter banished my children to the island of Anthemoessa to live forever. It was too much for their father and I.

We separated. I went to spend some time with them on the island. A lot of the time after the incident I traveled back to Olympus while their father stayed on the island with them. The girls learned to care for themselves as time passed. Their physical appearance and antics had by now earned them to be labeled as sirens of the sea. They were doomed to sing forever to call for Persephone. Demeter thought that wherever Persephone was taken, she would hear her companions singing and find her way home. They began to appear to and sing to sailors passing by who would become temporarily hypnotized. The sailors would crash their boats on Anthemoessa's rocky shore in their distraction. Stories grew among ships captains warning all to stay clear of the island and the sirens. This caused Aglaope later in life to begin to wander as far as she dared. She craved company. Aglaope did not want to be alone. Demeter had stopped caring by then as the ordeal of Persephone resolved itself later in years with the discovery of Demeter's own brother being the one to kidnap her daughter, taking Persephone as a wife. Persephone by this time resigned herself to this fate. Demeter never lifted the banishment.

    I felt that this alone was the worst tragedy in my immortal life. It is that incident that made me who I am today. I was born on this earth as a Muse of Song. I was sought after for the rapturous state I left those who would hear my melodious sounds. Now I am labelled as the Muse of Tragedy. Sadness wells up inside and bursts from me in a song that makes even the birds weep. The birds weep for relief from ever hearing it again. This sadness I feel inside is heavy and dark, a feeling of emptiness and longing for my lost daughters. I have to sing to let this darkness escape or it will devour me and I will be lost in it forever. I know they still live, but Hannah, the innocent girls Demeter sent to search the underworld did not return. What returned is the same as something that is of the underworld."

Hannah felt her hand reaching to brush away a fallen tear. "I had no idea Mel, I am so sorry."

"Hannah, I have learned to live this way. What we, you and I, must do is travel to Anthemoessa to confront my daughter, Aglaope. She is the one who stole the peace Jack should have in death. She owns his soul. Jack's soul can not become part of the cosmos unless it is released from where Aglaope has placed it in the underworld. It won't bring your husband back but you can help me to convince her from ever leaving the island again. The girls are unstable. They have been isolated there on the island for a very long time."

"Mel, how would I go to this place, this island? It isn't on any map I have seen. What is this gate you speak of to the underworld? Your daughter would kill me too."

"Hannah, I will take you to this island. There is more than one gate to the underworld. There are many gates. There is one on Anthemoessa and one close to my home on the Achelous River. In old times there were thousands of gates but now a lot of them are covered over. This is due to people encroaching into forests everywhere on earth. Some gates are covered by buildings but they still exist. We will retrieve Jack's soul for burial. I owe you this much because of what my daughter has done to your husband. I will care for you on the island. I will teach you the quick flight and how we travel this way. I can teach you a temporary complete layering to help aide you in our endeavour to attain the ability for short term for the flight for you. There is much more I have to tell you, but I want you to rest here for a few days. I must go to Olympus to see my family and ask for help on Anthemoessa. When I return I will familiarize you with more information about the history of my father's family. I will tell you about his sisters and brothers."

7

Hannah spent the next few days trying to sort out just where life was taking her. It was a short few months ago that she sat quietly reading "Wuthering Heights" over again, missing Jack. She was discussing with Ellie about where the next stage of her life was going to take her. When Hannah closed up the house in Forgotten Cove she felt her life would never be the same. This summer had turned out to be mind altering for her. The idea that some people are immortal and that the gods really did exist long ago and still do exist was still very foreign to her. What was next? Hannah had hugged Ellie and set out for the unknown. One thing Hannah did know for sure is that since she met Mel, the nightmare dreams of Jack calling for her, of her being on the boat seeing the sea killing him had now stopped. This definitely was tied up with Mel, but how? Did Mel's daughter Aglaope really layer her so roughly that her memory was now inside of Hannah? Was it Aglaope or Mel who somehow sent her to Jacks fishing boat or was it one of them on the boat? It did not make sense. What would Melpomene talk to her about next? Would Mel show her this layering and quick travel she was talking about? Hannah thought about these concepts as she stared at the setting sun, huge and blazing orange, sinking into the Red Sea. She felt a strange sense of exciting anticipation mixed with fear but definitely felt she trusted Mel. Hannah thought to herself that she must trust Mel. It would be her answer to why Jack died. Why did Jack die?

Melpomene arrived at the sanctuary high on Olympus. She greeted her Muse sisters, some of whom were also visiting. She greeted her mother, Mnemosyne, the Titaness, whose great beauty would never fade. Her memory was of all time past, present and the future. Mother could read the Akashic record. The Akashic record was the record Mother Earth kept of all time. Very few could read it or even knew of it. Those who could read it were carefully chosen as stewards of the earth. Mnemosyne was one of the chosen. This not only gave her the ability to see the past, the present and the future but to alter it in a mind of a human or animal. A mind was altered to keep an animal or human from the experience of pain too great to bear. This was how Mnemosyne used the altering. She could also alter happiness of those she chose.

Mnemosyne, Mel's mother was a guardian to the gates into the underworld. When a person was entering the gate, Mnemosyne would take away all of the pleasant memories of their time on earth. This ensured the time spent in the underworld was the suffering it was intended to be.

Zeus, Mel's father, was not home on Olympus when she visited today. He had many other shared families and obligations to his position as god of Olympus. Mel and her sisters, the other eight muses understood that this was normal for them, the way life would always be for them as daughters of Zeus.

Mel conveyed to her mother and sisters what had happened to Hannah by Aglaope's hand. She told them of her suspicions of

Aglaope leaving Anthemoessa many times. Mel told them of Aglaope taking and keeping the soul of Jack Gallegar. Calliope added to the conversation that people as far as the North Sea had been talking of seeing a siren of the sea. Stories of seeing even one siren haunt every fishwife. Sometimes more than one siren is seen, calling the ships to the rocky shores. Mother added that the girls, Mel's daughters, are restless. They knew that Demeter should have released them from their island long ago.

Persephone, her daughter had actually agreed to marry her kidnapper, Haides, long ago after he offered her control of the underworld with all of the riches Persephone desired. Persephone had become greedy and bitter with all she saw in the underworld. She agreed to spend time in the underworld, sharing time at home with her doting mother, Demeter. Persephone's return to her mother every year signaled spring with the earth awakening from the winter death Demeter gave it as punishment for Haides kidnapping Persephone. It was a powerful spell that could never be removed.

Mnemosyne looked sternly at Melpomene. "I know that you intend to take this Hannah to Anthemoessa to find Aglaope and confront her. What good will come of this? You could do this without involving Hannah. Have you thought of retrieving the soul to return to Hannah at the villa?" Mnemosyne knew as she was saying this to Mel that it was indeed Hannah's destiny to accompany the muses to the underworld.

"Do you forget that my daughters all share one mind with me and you are one of my daughters? I know what you think at all times. Your intention is honorable toward Hannah but she is a human, therefore, completely mortal. Hannah is not a match for Aglaope who wants her own way in this matter."

Mel felt she should justify her actions, "I want to convince Aglaope to return this tormented soul to its rightful grave. I have learned that the soul is still waiting at the River Styx for Persephone to decide its fate. It should be laid to rest since it was not an evil human that needed a lesson in the underworld. Hannah's dreams will stop completely when her husband's soul is at peace. She is having nightmares. Some of them are of her being on the fishing boat the night her husband was taken. Her mind is fragmenting into bits. Aglaope layered her very roughly. Hannah's mind has mixed with bits of Aglaope's memory and what Aglaope remembers of that night. I know Aglaope layered her to see how she would react to the pain of her husband's death. I want to know why. Why did she choose Hannah?"

Mnemosyne answered that things had never been good between Mel and her daughter Aglaope, who was more like her father. She was strong willed and ruthless like Achelous. Mnemosyne went on to say the record of life for Hannah does in fact read that Hannah was supposed to be part of their lives for awhile. Mnemosyne told her daughters the reason would reveal itself soon. Mnemosyne also told Mel that Hannah was chosen by Aglaope because of her very resemblance to Mel.

Mel wanted things to ease between her and her daughter Aglaope. Mel and Calli hoped to convince Demeter to release her three daughters from their punishment. This may be enough reason to Aglaope to stop being so defiant toward Mel and her sisters. All of the immortals have powers but it would be rare for one of them to interfere with one another's will. That is the reason the three daughters of Melpomene and Achelous were doomed to the island of flowers. It would mean dishonor to any person in Zeus' family to defy their Aunt Demeter.

Mnemosyne went on to warn her daughter Mel of the danger involved if this Hannah person should not be under her control at all times. She must be completely given over to Melpomene's layering not just willing to be layered but in a state of complete submission. This must be so Hannah would not have a will of her own while in quick flight. Mnemosyne warned Mel that the danger was having Hannah in a state of not having complete control of herself so could be taken over by anyone who can layer. Anthemoessa Island has a door to the underworld. Any of the underlings may be around to try to distract Mel in order to capture Hannah, a living soul. They would take her to the underworld to give her to Haides in exchange for favors. The danger is great for this Hannah, the mortal. The outcome would be a living death which was worse than Jack her dead husband's present existence.

8

Arabella summoned Hannah in the late afternoon three days later. Her mistress, Melpomene was requesting Hannah's presence. She had returned. Hannah and Mel greeted each other as sisters would. They both felt at ease with the other's company. Mel introduced Hannah to a woman who resembled Mel very much. The woman seemed to be the same age as Mel to Hannah. Her skin glowed as if it were the finest porcelain. She was a little taller and had an air of confidence that said she was all-knowing. The woman knew that she was perfection.

"Hannah, This is my sister muse, Calliope. She will assist us in our preparations for our venture into the underworld. Calli has offered to deal with my Aunt Demeter. We will to ask her to stop tormenting my daughters whenever they leave Anthemoessa Island by allowing them a little privacy in their wanderings. Calli will assist me to layer into you enough that you trust me to be one with you. As we progress with this type of deep layering Calli will assess you to see if you are layered enough to come with me to the island. With this assessment she will check to see that you have focused in the layer so completely that any outside distractions will not affect you. You and I will work on perfecting the trust I need from you to layer you so deeply that you give me complete control over you. When we have gained the trust, we will ask Calli to observe us. This way, you will not feel the flight to the island but you will see it all the same as you see what happens in a dream. Hannah, I only ask for your complete trust."

"Mel, I will do whatever I must for Jack to be at peace. I do trust you."

During the next week Hannah learned that she must open her heart and mind to Melpomene. She began to feel the gentle warmth in Melpomene's mind. Hannah felt as a baby being safely held in her mother's arm without any fear. This was a place Hannah wanted to stay. It removed the outside world from her mind. She became a part of Mel's mind in the place Mel kept sacred for her wolf, a sanctum of gentle warm breezes filled with the peace of childhood innocence.

Calliope left the villa a week later to contact Demeter at her home in Eleusis. Calli had become an adept with the gifts her father Zeus had bestowed upon her which included the gift of speaking in a manner that all listeners believed that her words were very important for them. She related very poetically to Demeter with the aid of conjuring the appropriate scenes, just how she, Demeter, had been so devastated with the loss of Persephone.

"Demeter, I remember so vividly how your motherhood was so violently assaulted the mournful day your own brother that you trusted with your very life stole your most precious possession, your innocent baby, Persephone." Demeter painfully re-lived her most intimate emotions from the day her innocent daughter was taken to be a bride for her own brother. Calli next showed Demeter that Melpomene suffered the same devastation with the banishment of her three daughters by Demeter to Anthemoessa, the island of flowers. "Melpomene weeps for the loss of her three babies. They will never be returned as the innocent children they once were. They have been returned to her as sirens, evil women from the underworld. When Melpomene weeps for her girls, the earth is sad and the clouds cover the sunshine."

Demeter's strong will only weakened enough to agree that the sirens should be allowed to leave the island for family visits to Mount Olympus. Only after Calli impressed upon Demeter just how devastated Persephone had been living without her, did visits to the River Achelous to their father for short periods get added to the new freedoms. Demeter pointed out that she was only agreeing since Haides, her own brother who had kidnapped her daughter, his own niece then married Persephone against her will, had at least allowed Persephone visits home to her mother. Demeter would agree the sirens could visit their parents. Demeter secretly believed that her other brother Zeus had been a part of this catastrophe even though it was Zeus who sent his favourite son, Hermes to rescue Persephone from Haides. She shared this with Calli. Calli hung her head and reassured Demeter this was not so. "Oh my dear Aunt Demeter, my father has always expressed his love for his niece, Persephone and for you also. I can assure you of it."

With this victory, a very pleased Calliope returned with the news to Melpomene at the villa in Jeddah.

Melpomene was relieved. She now had the ammunition to get Aglaope to release Jacks soul. The soul was to be taken back to Forgotten Cove. Mel told Calli that she had successfully layered deep enough into Hannah to take over completely, enabling her to rapid travel to Anthemoessa several times. Calliope spent the next week at the villa watching and assessing how deeply into Hannah Mel would layer. Melpomene was right. Hannah allowed her sill to be opened to this deep layering. Mel went in, taking over the conscious mind of Hannah completely, thus allowing her to share the experiences Mel was having.

"We must discuss one important issue," Mel told Hannah over late tea a few evenings before the departure to the island of flowers. "My daughter Aglaope may appear hostile toward you at first meeting. You are never to respond to this hostility. I will take care of that response. Whatever you hear is what you will hear through me and so I will answer. What you experience while layered is partially my experience since you will be layered by me. You will experience what I hear, see and feel. In essence you will see what I see but remain in your own body. Your body will still possess all of its own senses. You will still taste and smell and see things that are not of this earth. I will still be myself too. I will control you similarly to the way we all control our fingers on our hands. That is, I am in control of you but you must move. Does this make sense?"

"Mel I trust you with my safety. It sort of makes sense and I will do as you need me to do," said Hannah assuredly. "Can anyone hurt me? Will I remember any of it when we return to the villa?"

Mel went on, "They will only hurt you if they hurt me. Because you are my layer and my host, you will appear as only my shadow to them. In the underworld there isn't any sunshine to cast a shadow and so you will not be seen by the inhabitants who reside there. If someone has a torch they can see my shadow and may try to harm me to get to you. I will remain out of harm's way in the shadows and let Calli and Aglaope deal with Persephone. If I sense danger we will immediately depart the underworld. I will not venture beyond the River Styx. This is the command from Zeus, my father."

"You will meet another of my muse sisters at Anthemoessa Island. She is one of my younger sisters. Thalia is light-hearted and for this reason Calli and I asked her to go on ahead of us to my daughters to stay with them until our arrival. Thalia will serve as a necessary distraction to the unfinished business between Hermes and Persephone. Thalia will also prepare my three daughters for what Demeter has decided to be their new lives. Two of my daughters, Pisinoe and Thelxiepia will have been told that they can leave as they wish. We have requested Aglaope to aide us in the retrieval of your husband's soul since it is her responsibility to deal with Persephone. Thalia has already given us the information that Aglaope gave your husband's soul to Persephone as a gift to bribe her. Aglaope wanted Persephone to convince her mother, Demeter to let her leave the island. Of course, this didn't work out. She left the soul at the ferryman's shack for Persephone, who will not take it across the river until she is told what price Aglaope will take for it. We must have Aglaope with us to have Persephone release and return Jack's soul to us. We will then return his soul for release to Forgotten Cove after we leave the island of flowers. Jack will join the great cosmos and be at peace forever."

Hannah felt the tears quickly spring to her eyes causing her to blink. "Mel, I can never thank you enough." She realized just how raw her emotional state was concerning Jack.

Melpomene did not answer immediately for she was busy thinking of what could happen if Persephone did not agree with Aglaope backing out of the bargain. Persephone could release the wrath of Haides and his minions upon them. Mel knew she would escape this, being an immortal and untouchable to this kind of attack, but Hannah would not be afforded this luxury. She stopped the next thought from forming.

9

The island of flowers was fragrant with the scent of honey from the flowers, even though it was now late November. A person could almost be smothered in the heady citrus and nutty aroma from the lemon, olive and almond trees. It rained flower petals from the orange trees that were forever blossoming and bearing fruit. Hannah tried to take in the beauty in her altered state. She felt as if she were in a very comfortable dream world, a place where she would like to stay forever. By contrast the shore line completely obliterated the cobalt blue sea. It was filled with huge boulders, sharp and in varying heights. It would be impossible to come here by boat. This island was totally inaccessible because of the jagged boulders on the shore that stood as the dominant feature of the island. Rock formations interspersed with bleached bones of those who did try and fail to come ashore to explore the island filled the outer edges of the island.

Hannah had researched whatever information she could find on the computer in her bedroom at the villa in Jeddah. There was not a lot of information about the island of flowers. It was called

Anthemoessa and a lot of flowers grew there. She was now familiar with the few stories of how sirens of the sea enticed ships with enchanting songs. Their haunting voices hypnotized the sailors who only found out too late that they had sailed off course.

Hannah tried to think of the short flight to the island but only remembered Mel telling her to hold her hands tightly. As practiced, Hannah immediately let go of her will to let herself become completely layered. Hannah felt the stillness inside of her. She heard the strong wind but did not sense any danger. She felt slight movements as they flew to the island from the Jeddah villa in a heartbeat. The island of Anthemoessa filled the senses. It was untouched by the outside world. Hannah looked in every direction at the blossoms falling gently to the earth. She inhaled the beauty in her attempt to commit it to a memory she could retrieve in the future.

When Hannah paused after this short adjustment, taking in the beauty of the meadows, she saw ahead of her who she guessed was Thalia talking with Calli and Mel. They were deep in conversation with their backs to her. They were speaking with a woman who was the image of Melpomene. It seemed that this family all bore a strong resemblance to each other. She approached them slowly in case the conversation was not for her ears.

The younger woman, the one they were speaking with, was Aglaope she guessed. She looked so identical to Mel. She was saying, "Mother you don't understand how lonely we were here on this isolated island. We wanted companions. That is why we lured all of those ships. We three sisters want to marry as others do and have the family life we deserve. You have stopped coming to visit and father has never come for years now. Thalia tells us that Demeter had a change of heart and has agreed we three can leave to visit Olympus and River Achelous. Thalia said Calli made the agreement with Demeter. It would be that I return back the gift I gave Persephone of the soul of that woman's husband". Aglaope pointed a finger at Hannah and stared right through her, repeating, "That woman standing behind you. Why did you bring her here?"

Hannah caught her breath as she remembered not to speak. She felt too frightened to talk and would not have been able to make sense. Mel looked at her.

"Hannah, be still, you are safe, this is my daughter Aglaope and my sister Thalia who you have not met as of yet. Thalia has explained to my three daughters what Demeter has decided, thanks be to Calli. Before Aglaope can also leave as Pisinoe and Thelxiepia have done, she must retrieve the soul of Jack so you can say your good-bye to him at last. His soul will be given to the sea where it left Jack's body in Forgotten Cove. Now let's take action. We must keep moving toward our destination in the underworld."

Aglaope continued to glare at Hannah even as Thalia grasped her by the shoulders and urged her to move onward.

The flowers at the gate to the underworld were not as lush as on the rest of the island. They were less fragrant with smaller blossoms. Somehow the green of the withered foliage at this gate looked uncared for. It did not thrive but cowered as if it sensed the evil beyond the gate. As they approached the gate to the underworld Hannah saw a man of unearthly beauty. He was waiting for them to arrive with such a charming smile for his visitors.

Here at the gate the travelers met Hermes, second youngest of the immortals that were the sons of Zeus. Hermes had been tasked to take the muse sisters as far as the River Styx. He could move freely in the underworld. Hermes could walk in both the immortal and mortal worlds. Hermes would escort and protect the muses and their new traveling companion. He did this not only out of fear of Zeus but as a duty. He was in awe of the father of the muses even though Zeus was his father too. The god Zeus tasked Hermes as a

the VILLA

protector for the traveler as well as for those who were shepherds of animals. Without introduction to Hannah the group entered through the gate. Hannah noted that although it was called a gate it was a nothing more than a cave-like hole large enough to walk through. It was covered in dead grasses, disguising it's entrance. Hannah wondered just how many wandered through it by accident until Mel answered by layering into her mind that no human has ever lived on the island aside from her daughters. The musky stench of decay was overpowering compared to the fragrant smells outside just a few feet away from here. The pathway to the River Styx was mostly in darkness. Hannah was a little relieved since she did not care to see what might be present with her inside this cavern making her feel so uncomfortable.

The ferryman on the River Styx had been previously warned by Zeus that he should never allow his daughters, the sister muses, to ride his ferry. They should never cross the River Styx. Zeus own brother was Haides, the god of the underworld. Even though it was his brother, Zeus had warned Haides that he would open the underworld and flood it with sunlight if this were to happen, if they were to ever cross the river. Haides knew this too be true. Hermes also knew this to be true. Zeus always kept his word. Haides wanted the underworld to stay in darkness, in shadows, away from sunlight. It was necessary for the survival of the underworld and the elements of darkness to be kept as such.

Hermes had spent a lot of his time learning from Calliope to become a very skilled negotiator in the art of persuasion. He also learned to quickly take control of a situation from Calli. Hermes spent some of his time on Olympus and fell in love with the muse sister Ourania. Although Hermes loved the muse sister Ourania and their child, he also had loved Persephone, the daughter of Demeter and wife of Haides. He had spent his younger years wooing Persephone whenever she returned to Demeter but she did not notice Hermes existed. He would make this journey hoping that Persephone would agree to the bargain Calli had made with her in return for soul of the earth woman's dead husband. The muses wanted Persephone to return the soul to them. The plan was to return the soul to its place of death so it could go to a final rest in the peace it rightfully should have. Calli would bargain even further in exchange for this one soul that the muses would help Persephone gain many unclaimed souls from the island of the Gorgons. Hermes agreed to join them on the island of the Gorgons. Hermes would aide Persephone in acquiring as many as one hundred souls. Hermes would do anything for Persephone's attention and her love.

Many years before today Persephone had lost sight of everything important in her life, she had replaced it with her greed for wealth. Persephone would try to acquire more souls than the many lost souls her husband Haides owned. She had become very competitive with Haides. It satisfied the bitterness of having him as her husband. Persephone did not choose this life but now relished in the fact that she could have anything she would ask Haides to give her.

Mel, her sisters and daughter chatted with Hermes as they walked slowly into the darkness. Hannah was not introduced to him until they had walked for nearly fifteen minutes. He looked into her eyes momentarily, and then looked away. It was enough time for Hannah to feel his interest in what brought her to this day. The only recurring thought Hannah had right now was of how much her nostrils felt completely assailed with the putrefaction. Almost immediately after entering the gate she smelled and saw abominations in the semi-darkness that defied the sanity of the logical mind. The inside walls of the cavern pulsed with black sticky ooze. At first Hannah thought the movement may have been a vertigo she developed from the quick flight. Hannah soon realized the movement that come from walls were the same movements as the beat of a heart. The wailing sounds she heard that day were not sounds from humans. They were the lament of life suffering in a living death. Release from this place for those inhabiting the realm here would never happen. It was hell. It was the underworld. Hermes led the entourage through the darkened and perilous landscape toward the dimly lit lantern of the ferryman. Hannah felt both of her hands held tightly in the grip of two of the sisters. She was firmly sandwiched between Melpomene and Thalia. Hermes walked on ahead with Aglaope and Calliope. Hannah distracted herself by watching Hermes. There was an aura about him that spoke to Hannah. He was undoubtedly the most beautiful man she had ever seen. Hannah felt disturbed by her own thoughts as Hermes turned to face her and stared into her eyes once again. She felt the magnetic pull of him. Hannah noticed how Hermes talked to the others in an animated way using movements from every part of his body. Hannah banished these thoughts in order to stay focused in her layer. She was here to retrieve the soul of Jack. She needed to stay focused as Mel had instructed her. Hermes was indeed light-hearted today. He knew he would meet Persephone at the ferry on the River Styx. The desolate landscape began to give up the putrid smell coming from the stagnant bubbling water. The travelers had now reached the River Styx after twenty minutes at the slow pace they moved to accommodate Hannah.

The ferryman stepped forward. Hannah could see that he was not completely a whole man. At one time maybe he was but now the ferryman sported open festering gashes on his head and face. He was missing almost all of his fingers. Hannah could see the stubs on the ends of his hands where fingers should be as he waved his hands around in animated conversation with Hermes. The ferryman's wounds would forever remain unhealed in this unhealthy environment. He was raggedly dressed. When he smiled at Hannah she saw blackened stubs of teeth. She saw hair that moved in the dim light. Hannah quickly averted her gaze not wanting to know why it moved.

The ferryman told Hermes they should board and he would take them on the ferry to Persephone. Hermes pulled himself up to his full stature. "Ferryman, don't be a fool. I will bring the wrath of Zeus himself to you and this damned place," he roared at the ferryman. "You were to bring Persephone to meet us here."

A throaty feminine laugh filled the fetid air. Persephone stepped from the shadows. Hannah blinked, adjusting her sight to better see the once innocent beautiful girl. Persephone showed signs of how the underworld wore a person down. She looked a little like one of the faded beauties of the great American southland. A rose needs the light to live or it will wither just as Persephone's beauty had withered without light.

Hannah knew this person had to be Persephone. No one else who lived here appeared alive enough to laugh. For the souls trapped here, that was forgotten long ago.

Hannah noticed Persephone held a small sack teasingly behind her back. Was Jack's soul in a bag? Is this all that is left of my husband? Hannah felt her heart beginning to race. Mel placed her strong capable arm around Hannah's shoulders and warned her not to react. Hannah felt numbness setting in. She thought of the wedding vows on the beach in Forgotten Cove. She remembered the evening walks along the beach holding the hand of the person who was her life. Just like Catherine, the heroine in "Wuthering Heights," Hannah didn't just love Jack when they married; she felt she had become Jack that day.

More distant laughter brought Hannah back into the present. Hannah looked up to see what was happening now. The sack was now in the hands of Aglaope. Hermes was deep in conversation with

Persephone. Mel was tugging at her arm, urging her to start walking back toward the gate that was the entrance to the underworld. The ground under Hannah's feet felt softened. She looked down and saw eyes looking back at her pleading for help. Hannah felt her mouth become dry as her mind quickly lost focus. She felt close to panic. This time it was Calli who grabbed her hand and told her to play it smart. Focus on the opening at the gate to the underworld. Hannah began to feel woozy. Both Mel and Calli half lifted her and moved forward at a quickened pace toward the light, the air and the beautiful meadow on the island of flowers.

The bright sun temporarily blinded Hannah's eyes as she felt the ground suddenly slam the air out of her lungs. Hannah heard someone talking but opted to welcome the cool darkness that soothed away the horrors she had experienced today.

10

Three luxurious months had passed at the villa. A lot had changed. Hannah had become weak from the stress brought on by the energy needed for the concentration she used to stay layered on the trip to Anthemoessa. The return trip to the villa was still blacked out from her memory. Feeling weakened from the ordeal, Hannah stayed in her quarters and kept to herself. Arabella became her constant companion, caring daily for her. The two shared stories of how although they lived worlds apart they had developed such a kinship with each other. Hannah felt most flattered by the undivided attention she had from Hermes. He had accompanied the muses back to the villa and set up residence for the last few months. Hermes golden brown locks and green eyes greatly outshone the nagging doubt Hannah felt because of the intense interest she had developed for him. Hermes sported a new aura of soft golden light. For whatever reason there was magnetic attractions toward this man, it made Hannah feel very little will to resist the pull toward him. She wanted male attention from him at this time in her life. Somehow it helped Hannah keep away the thoughts of the underworld. Hannah felt it was time to move on and let Jack be the beautiful memory he had become. Hermes loved the way Hannah reminded him of the same innocent characteristics the muses had as young girls when he visited them on Olympus. She made him feel alive. Arabella made Hermes feel this way too. Arabella was so much like her ancestor Hayghar. Hermes had also loved Hayghar years before either Arabella or Hannah was born. Hermes had loved a lot of women in his life. Neither Arabella nor Hannah knew or cared to know the business Hermes had with the other. They just knew that Hermes made them happy. Hannah grew strong again. Her thoughts turned to home and the steep bluffs that protected Forgotten Cove. She remembered the wonderful little house where she hoped to raise children with Jack. Hannah thought of her friend Ellie who was probably frantic with worry of her whereabouts. Hannah longed for home. She felt an initial stirring deep inside of her. It was time to nest.

There was word of Aglaope finally finding someone who cared about her. This information came to Hannah from Arabella. Mel confided to Arabella that her daughter Pisinoe mentioned to her they thought Aglaope was with child. Mel seemed very pleased that her wayward daughter may soon make her a grandmother. The three sat in the garden in the evening breeze when Hannah decided to tell Mel that perhaps it was time for her to leave the villa to return home to Forgotten Cove. They discussed further how and where Aglaope would meet Hannah with the sack containing Jack's soul. Hannah felt this was her opportunity to get the answers for a few questions she had for Melpomene concerning Jack.

"Mel, what is actually in this sack? Why can't I carry it home?" Hannah began her questions.

She was answered by Mel after a full minute's silence. "Hannah, you can't see anything in this sack. What is inside is a form of energy left over from the life of Jack Gallegar. When I say you can't see anything in the sack, it doesn't mean that an immortal can't see what is inside. We immortals see with all our senses, including what you would refer to as the sixth sense. In that sack, layered into the fabric is the person you knew as Jack. It must be safeguarded by someone such as an immortal. The reason for this is because they know it is there inside the sack whereas a mortal may think of it as an empty sack and toss it aside. Hannah, have you ever had a feeling that someone is in the room with you although it is an apparent empty room? This is a traveling soul passing by. Perhaps the soul chose to be with you or perhaps it was discarded in that room. Aglaope will be tasked with carrying this soul to hand over to you on the dock in Forgotten Cove. This way the soul can be close to where it left its earthly body so it can see that it must now leave this body it has become separated from. It must leave for the great cosmos to join those who have moved on before them. Does this help you to understand a little easier?"

"A little," was the answer from Hannah to Mel, "Mel, why did I dream of being on the fishing boat and sometimes dream of standing on shore watching the boat go down in several of my different dreams?"

"Hannah, do you remember when I taught you to open up your mind for me so that I could enter your mind and layer you? That is because you agreed and were receptive. When a host like you is not prepared or not receptive we can still layer them. Aglaope did that to you. She wanted to experience your reaction to seeing Jack die. She felt you reminded her somehow of me and that she would get to me by punishing you. I know that will not make sense but at the time she was looking for a soul to barter with Persephone to get Demeter to give her some freedoms away from the island. When she saw how much you resembled me she felt it would be a type of revenge for her being stuck on the island all of her life. Somehow she blames me for not getting her freedom from Demeter's punishment earlier. Aglaope wanted to see how you felt at that moment of Jack's death so she layered into your mind roughly. We sit on a sill like a window sill and when it opens we enter gently. What Agloape did to you was to break the window and enter without permission. This caused bits of her memory to be left behind in your mind. You dreamed of what Aglaope saw the night of Jacks death."

"That answers a lot about the strange dreams. The dreams are gone, Mel. I sleep so peacefully since coming to the villa. I have much to think about when I return back to Forgotten Cove". Hannah felt tired.

"Hannah, we will arrange flights, connections and a driver for you to meet Aglaope in Forgotten Cove. You must rest tonight. If I don't see you before you leave, please know that I will visit you in the next few months to check on your health." Melpomene watched Hannah closely with a small smile as Hannah rubbed her abdomen.

11

Ellie arose from a warm bed late that morning. She begrudgingly opened the small book store after two cups of very hot coffee. It was pointless to expect a lot of business during this season except for the rare local wandering in to complain about the long cold winter. Ellie had created a very lucrative online business selling her books and writing articles to create interest for her readers living in the area. It was late February. The weather was always coldest outside nearer to the water. Bitter wind coming in from the Atlantic invaded every space and cut deep into your bones. She could see the salt-water waves, forever unfrozen, white-capping as they pounded the wharf. Forgotten Cove had a mix of salt and fresh water because of its proximity to the ocean. Salt water waves never froze over like the lakes inland and so winter on the ocean never created a magic frozen wonderland. There were huge expanses of ice where fresh water had frozen over, creating rock like projections along the shoreline. Instead of winter beauty, greyness hangs over the landscape until spring when the earth turns to see the sun again.

Ellie spotted the lone figure at the end of the dock only because it moved.

"What a fool," Ellie said aloud, "Does that person not understand the danger on that old wooden dock with the wind blowing at it so hard."

It was icy and they could slip off the edge very easily. The person appeared to be throwing something into the water. As Ellie debated whether to put on a jacket and walk down to the frigid waters edge or to scream at the person from the warmth of her house to get off of the dock, the lone figure turned and walked toward her and the book shop.

"Oh my God," screamed Ellie," it's Hannah."

Ellie forgot just how cold the weather was today. She scrambled out the door to greet her dear friend. Hannah saw Ellie coming toward her as they got closer to each other. They hugged as only great friends would hug. Tears freezing on their faces made them laugh at the silliness of how quickly the frozen tears formed.

"Hannah, of all people who should know to stay off of that icy dock in winter, you should know. It's covered in ice." Ellie's blued lips chattered from the cold as she tried to warm herself from the very few minutes she had spent outside in the frigid air.

"Oh Ellie, it is so good to be back home. Let's get inside and make some hot cocoa to drink. I have a lot to tell you," replied Hannah.

"Hannah, first things first, what in hell were you doing on the dock?" Ellie was hardly listening to what Hannah was saying.

"Ellie like I said, I have a lot to tell you but before I come in to visit you, I needed to go to the dock to do something I should have done years ago. I tossed my "Wuthering Heights" into the Bay. I will no longer hang onto yesterday with its sadness."

"Well, that is a step forward, although I could have sold it for you. Why could it have not waited for a warmer day?" queried the still shivering Ellie.

"I will tell you everything but let's get warmed first," Hannah shivered back at Ellie.

Ellie went to the kitchen to prepare two very hot cocoa drinks for them to sip on while they talked.

A short time before high noon Hannah had watched the dog-eared book disappear into the waves. The evening before this Hannah had watched as the sack containing Jack's soul was quickly eaten up in the same waves. Aglaope had a car and driver for Hannah when she got off of the airplane in Montreal. Through a lot of uneasy silences in the conversation and even more uneasy silence when discussing Melpomene, Aglaope had escorted Hannah all the way back to Forgotten Cove. It was agony for both of them. They hardly spoke but Aglaope seemed to welcome a chance to be anywhere but Anthemoessa. Hannah had air traveled by private charter, then this limousine all the way to Forgotten Cove. It was a kind gesture of care from Mel. Aglaope would later fast travel back to Olympus to let her mother know it was over, the soul of Jack finally placed at rest back in Forgotten Cove. Aglaope was tasked to bring the retrieved soul back to the place from where she had taken it. It was Aglaope who caused this two day storm to suddenly descend on Forgotten Cove while she finished turning over the sack to Hannah. This storm with frigid temperatures was provided by Aglaope so she could be assured of privacy by keeping the locals indoors while she was returning the soul. Aglaope tried to be humorous by telling Hannah she promised she wouldn't sing today. It was meant to be funny. Hannah didn't react.

Aglaope looked at Hannah and said, "You know you do look like her - my mother. Maybe I will behave a little differently toward her now that I have gained some freedom. Through my new freedom Hannah, I met a sailor from the orient. I will join him again on his cargo ship when I leave you. Now let's return this soul and move on. I will go to Olympus to see my mother and tell her the news of my sailor friend. You know Hannah; you will always remain a mortal. Don't forget that in the next few months when you are alone without your Hermes around."

Aglaope handed the sack to Hannah. Hannah felt the weight of the sack like a feather slide quickly from her hands.

She said quietly, "Good-bye my Heathcliffe." She would think of her beautiful memories and love of Jack, alone, later this evening. Hannah thought about the bitter sweetness of this act of release. Hannah spent the night thinking of her fast second goodbye to Jack. She thought about how Aglaope tried to create conversation with her. Hannah slept late in the night and arose with the decision to put her copy of "Wuthering Heights" to rest in the sea to ensure that she would never spend another summer reading it.

Hannah now refocused her attention back to Ellie and to today.

"Ellie, I am going to live my life fully, from today moving forward, each day," smiled Hannah.

"Hannah, tell me, what has happened? Did you meet someone? Your acting silly like a school girl, the way you acted when you first met Jack." Ellie teased.

Hannah inhaled deeply, placing her hand on her abdomen as she felt the tiny flutter, a feeling similar to butterflies moving, gently exploring their new home inside of her.

"Well, I have moved on just like we discussed last summer before I went overseas to join Mel. I have learned to place Jack in a special place in my life, Ellie. He is a memory that will always be a happy part of my past. Jack will always be with me in some way."

Hannah glanced toward the sea as if the sea could hear her words, as if the tiny sack containing the last of her beloved Jack might feel betrayed by hearing of her encounters with Hermes.

"One more thing Ellie, this August I will make you a godmother to the very reason I am so happy today. Ellie, I am pregnant! I am having a baby in about five, close to six months from now."

12

The month of August came to Forgotten Cove and went again for more than a decade and a half. With this passing also came the happiest years of Hannah's life. With each year passing Hannah and Ellie become closer with sharing the small daughter of Hannah. Ellie knew of the very handsome caller that frequented Hannah and her daughter Lily's home. He was of course, Lily's father. This handsome man called Hermes attended to every need of the little girl as she blossomed from a curious wide-eyed child into a beautiful young woman. This young woman, this old soul, talked of places unheard of and of times past that she had not lived to experience. Lily seemed to know of many events that were very esoteric in their nature. She spoke of living in long ago times as if she had extracted them from her own memory. Lily talked of the caves deep in the Himalayan Mountains of Tibet. Ellie could see in those early years that Lily had outgrown the small village of Forgotten Cove before her pre-teen years. Ellie noticed the other frequent visitor to Hannah's house. She was that beautiful woman, the very same woman that Hannah met all those years ago on the beach, the woman who took Hannah away to far off lands. This woman, Mel, was a relative of Lily's father and so she was also a part of Lily's family. Some of this information Hannah kept to herself at first. It was on the long winter nights as Lily was growing up, Hannah did share pieces of her new family with Ellie. Some of this information never quite made sense to Ellie.

Every school day Ellie watched for the small girl in the direction of the new part of Forgotten Cove to see Lily wandering along in private conversation. She was talking to herself while walking home from school as she did since Lily started attending the local school all those years ago.

Today the late day sun looked huge as it lazed in the western sky. The shadows were growing longer earlier in the day. Lily looked to the northwest, watching a lone figure standing on the bluffs. She sensed rather than knew when she was being watched. Lily felt a sense of being watched ever since she was a small girl. Lately with the frequent talks mother and Ellie were having with her, Lily thought she might know why she had always felt this way. The time was coming nearer for Lily to be taken to meet the rest of the family. Her mother sat with her on cold winter nights recounting her life married to Jack, telling Lily how happy she was back then. Lily knew that Jack was not her father since she was four years old.

Lily knew from a young age the information given to her from her mother about her father made him very different than her friend's fathers. He was not the same as the ordinary dads the rest of her friends at school had. From the visits with her father Lily realized that not all people were the same. Some people, including her, had powers to sense danger and to know what others were thinking. Mother said she had inherited this keen perception from Aunt Mel. Sure, she watched the illusions of famous people in Las Vegas but was mildly impressed with their performances. Lily was more intrigued with the effects the illusions had on the people in an audience. They wanted to believe. She sensed this. Her mom even took her to see a special magic show in New York. Lily realized at that time as a small child that she could feel and see what others were thinking, even control it a little by appropriate comments at the right time. This made it more exciting.

Lily was gifted with a beautiful singing voice as a small girl. Teachers at her school made her the star of any event the school had as a concert for the people of Forgotten Cove.

Growing up in Forgotten Cove meant that Lily spent a lot of her free time wandering the high bluffs alone above Forgotten Cove. Lily would try to see the end of the ocean as if by staring at the ocean it would show her its other shore, many days distant travel from Forgotten Cove. Saturday was her favourite day. Saturday meant a day free from school. That was a day she always spent at Ellie's book shop. Lily had probably read every book in the store plus all of the e-books Ellie let her download to her tablet. Most of the books would never be of interest to the simple nature of people in Forgotten Cove. The books Lily read were different. Lily had read books by authors people in Forgotten Cove had never heard of. The books written by authors on their memory of past lives were some of her favourite books.

Lily loved the surrounding forests and ocean close to her home. Her young fingers had turned every page of the goldmine Ellie possessed in National Geographic magazines. The forests close to Forgotten Cove were filled with the wildlife and the wild flowers from the pages of these National Geographic magazines. Lily felt very fortunate to have this beautiful spot on earth as home. She often sat on the bluffs singing into the wind, listening to her own voice as the wind picked it up and carried it to distant lands. Lily would imagine that others could hear her singing even thousands of miles from Forgotten Cove. Lily realized too that very few people she knew had her endurance to run as she would run for hours at a time. She was fast and sure footed. Mother said this was an inherited gift too, her father's gift to her.

Lily blinked, realizing that she was daydreaming again and staring directly at the sun now barely visible as it set over the distant tree tops in the west. She looked back toward the bluffs and noticed the lone figure that stood on the bluff earlier was now gone. Sometimes she thought it was her father. Lily loved the way he was always around taking extra time to care for her. Sometimes the figure on the bluffs looked like a woman. From this distance it was not easy to be sure. Aunt Melpomene comes to visit her and mother often, usually every couple of weeks to see progress with her niece. This figure in robes had to be her. She could see the long flowing robes on the figures on the bluff but most of the time with the sun shining so brightly on them high above her; she could only make out a shape so never really knew if it were a man or woman who watched over her. Everyone in her father's family wore long robes so Lily never really knew just who was watching her from the bluffs above Forgotten Cove.

13

While growing up in Forgotten Cove, Lily and her mother spent a great deal of time at Ellie's house. Mother seemed very content sharing everything with Ellie as her closest friend. Every event life brought to Lily and Hannah was a joy to Ellie's ears. Ellie was godmother to Lily. She was sensible and Lily could see how she kept her mother grounded. Ellie gave mother advice on raising a daughter in Forgotten Cove. When Lily was seven she realized she could do things that other children could not do. Lily had a discussion with her mother about some of her talents such as knowing what others were thinking before they spoke. Hannah told Lily not to tell other children what she was capable of doing since their parents may feel it to be odd behavior. Lily was typical as any child but as curious as any adult. She discovered layering at about seven and one half years old while playing in a meadow filled with wildflowers high up on the bluffs. Lily loved the brown and orange colors of the devils paintbrush and the shiny petals of the yellow buttercups. One day while looking into a buttercup she discovered a small black bug trying to climb out. It just wandered around the inside of the flower without being able to climb the slippery walls. Lily tried to communicate to the small bug by thinking that it should slow down and think about going between the petals to climb the rough backside of the petal and find its way out. Soon she had stepped inside the thoughts of the bug. The flower was quite sticky on the surface so Lily started moving toward the centre of the flower. Here she found the tall cylindrical columns covered in an even stickier powdered substance that might be easier to climb. As she was attempting to climb up one column she became aware of a loud roaring noise above her. Lily looked up to see a furry yellow and black monstrosity coming into the flower. Horrified at this, Lily slammed back into herself away from the mind of the bug in time to see a bee sitting on the buttercup she held in her hand. She threw down the flower to run home and tell her mother what happened high on the bluff that day, laughing all the way down the steep embankment.

This was Lily's first awakening with her layering talent. Hannah invited Mel to come to visit and explain what layering was to her daughter. Mel laughed as Lily explained the terror she felt as the bee wanted to simply perform its pollen transport duty in nature providing honey for the hive. Mel told her of trying to layer birds when she was a child, how they never would sit still long enough for Mel to find a sill in order to enter the birds mind. Lily was still young so Mel advised her to take her time with rabbits and house pets for now.

Growing up in Forgotten Cove also meant spending summers on the shore of the ocean digging for clams or simply gathering odd shapes of driftwood for her mother's or Ellie's garden. Shortly after Lily turned fourteen she layered another human for the first time. It was a day Lily would forever keep close to her heart. It was a beautiful late summer afternoon. Lily decided to take a walk down

the VILLA

to the shoreline to see if there were any tourists visiting in Forgotten Cove she had not yet encountered. She saw a family with a young boy in a wheel chair. He was sitting watching the sunlight dance on the waves. The parents were busy in conversation so Lily decided to say hello to the boy who appeared to be around her age. It quickly become obvious the boy did not live in this world. He lived in his own world inside his mind. Lily invited herself in. She stepped carefully onto the window sill and saw the vast amount of unused space beyond it. She could hear him crying out to have some memories placed in these empty spaces. Lily knew she must move slowly in this unexplored mind. She asked him to let her give him some of her own memories of running on the bluffs. He hesitantly consented as she held his hand for reassurance. When she stepped gently into the vacuous space in the trapped boy's mind, Lily stared into his eyes and remembered times she was running through the fields of flowers up on the bluffs until she thought her lungs would burst. She felt the sun touching her, feeling so hot on her skin that it started to bring sweat to her brow sending tiny rivulets trickling down to sting her eyes. Lily smelled the salty sea, listening to it as it pounded the rocks. She could see it sending cascades of white water up the bluff. Lily listened to the birds and crickets as they became agitated from her disturbing their restful summer afternoon while she was running through the fields. Lily laughed out loud as she run back down the bluffs tumbling head over heels scattering long grasses and flowers in every direction.

A voice interrupted her, "Young lady, what are you doing to my son?"

Lily stopped and focused on the boy's mother away from the boy's mind. "I was just trying to talk with him to cheer him up."

Again his mother spoke, questioning her, "My son has not spoken since his accident. I heard two of you children laughing but you are here alone. I thought I heard him laughing with you. Could this be true? I know he doesn't understand or respond to us. Maybe it was an unconscious reaction to see such a small girl like you, someone he has never seen before. He has only been in the company of adults, not children. Excuse us. We will leave now so please be on your way."

"Yes, sorry ma'am, I didn't mean to make a problem." Lily whispered and walked home thinking of what had just happened. She realized that she could do it. Lily could layer another human. She felt like the world could become hers now. Today Lily realized the joy she could give to others, people just like this boy who were just spectators in the world. Lily could see inside the minds of other humans, not just small animal's minds. Today was a happy day for Lily. She knew she had given the boy in the wheel chair a joyful place he could visit over and over again. He did laugh aloud at her falling down the sandy bluffs, looking silly as she spat sand from her mouth. Lily was confident that he now would have a happy place of his own forever to retreat into from the outside. He would have his very own memory forever.

LILY'S FAVORITE AUNT WAS AUNTIE Mel or Melpomene. Lily would walk the lonely bluffs with Mel. This was their private time. Lily felt she could tell Mel anything she felt inside, all of her hopes and dreams. Mel never thought Lily was a silly girl, rather treated her as the young woman she had become. The conversations had lately become mainly about all of the cities Mel wanted to take Lily to visit one day. Mel and Lily would sit at the top of the bluffs together and sometimes they would sing together. It would begin with a faint melodic hum that they would share with the small animals in the area. These small animals would listen intently. Lily could feel the communication with them. Sometimes the local brush wolves would sit with Mel. Lily loved the way they looked into Mel's eyes as she stroked their fur. On one lazy afternoon a young bear cub, tired from play, had come to sleep at Mel's feet while she sang perfect notes that seemed to soothe him just as his mother would. Lily laughed uncontrollably when the surprised cub woke up and realized that it was not his mother stroking his fur. The cub quickly retreated into the forest looking back to see if they were behind him. Lily loved the memories of those afternoons. The two harmonized their voices lifting them to the wind. The wind carried the voices on it's currents to share with the inhabitants of the forest nearby. Those were the long summer days that turned into beautiful memories and built an unspoken bond of complete trust between the two.

14

One day after school had ended for the summer break mother announced that she was taking Lily to Saudi Arabia this year. Hannah seemed a little sad when she told Lily that Mel's family said it was necessary for Lily to come. Mother had told Lily of Arabella and her daughter, Qamar. This was great news to Lily that Qamar was actually her half sister. Apparently there was a part of the family living in a villa in Jeddah that rivaled any palace on earth. Lily had been told that part of her extended family would include two relatives close to her age. She was to meet these family members for the first time in Jeddah. One of them was her half sister, Qamar who was the daughter of the housekeeper, Arabella. Mother had told her stories while she was growing up of how Arabella's family had always been part of Aunt Mel's family. Qamar lived at the villa where she was home schooled. She was tutored on the refinements of a being young lady. Qamar was half sister to Lily because the father of Qamar was her father, Hermes. Mother did not want to talk to her about this situation too deeply until Lily was much older. Lily could see that the subject made her mother feel a bit uncomfortable.

the VILLA

The other family member she was to meet was another relative named Ikram. Ikram was the daughter of Aglaope who was Aunt Mels's daughter. Aglaope was the woman who had been somehow involved in the death of Lily's mother's first husband. This made Lily confused of why they would want to be in the same house as her but never the less Lily was eager to meet her and her daughter Ikram. Lily was thinking that this family seemed to call everyone a "cousin" who was a member of the family. They seemed like such a huge family. Melpomene had already told Lily when she was around eight years old that she was born into a family who were children of Zeus. This was easy for her to accept as a young child. Just as they were, she too was a descendant of Zeus. Anyone else may find all of this unbelievable and a little sinister, maybe even a little crazy but Lily learned through the years it did not matter what others thought, this was her family. Lily was taught while growing not to share and did not share this information at her school.

On visits from her father Lily learned further from him what layering was all about. She also learned of the historical fame of her father's family. Her fathers' family all seemed to have great musical and writing talents. Lily's father told her that she would some day spend her time at the villa perfecting her amateur skills in layering. She was told that the family matriarch would teach her how to decrease the time in which it takes a person to travel anywhere on earth they wanted to travel. Distance would not matter. Lily was really looking forward to this traveling especially so far away from Forgotten Cove. Finally the time had come for her journey. She had been to Montreal and New York with mother and Ellie. Lily was the envy of the other school children who knew that one winter vacation she went to Las Vegas with mother and Ellie to see the famous magicians. Now she was to travel to Saudi Arabia. It seemed so exotic to Lily. It was a country that held many secrets. This intrigued

Lily. Her mother didn't seem as excited as she was about it. In fact, she seemed very distracted lately. It was as if something was really weighing heavy on her mind.

The great resemblance in the physical appearances of Lily and her mother was mentioned by all people who met them. Lily looked a lot like her mother with long wavy brown tresses streaked golden from the sunlight. She was tiny limbed but very strong. Her eyes were pale grey with flecks of green light. Mother said they were her father's eyes. The kids at school would tell her they were cat's eyes. Lily laughed at this as she made her way home from the bluffs. She wanted to talk to her mom about the trip. Lily would ask her mom after the evening meal tonight about what seemed to be on her mind lately.

Days later aboard the Saudia Airlines flight from JFK to Jeddah, Lily thought about the conversation she had with her mother concerning this trip to the villa. Hannah told Lily she would learn things that others thought to be impossible to do. The immortals could travel to different parts of earth in mere minutes. They could meet people from different time periods. She told Lily that her extended family members of pure blood were ageless. Hannah confided to Lily that she did not know if Lily was ageless too. This was the reason mother was so distracted. It was what seemed to be bothering her mother. Her daughter was a half mortal. Lily's mother was afraid that she would never see her daughter grow old and have children like other parents see. Mother was afraid that Lily would be off somewhere in a distant land living a life that her mother could never be part of. Lily told her mother that nothing on earth could ever separate them. Lily assured her mother that she would always be a part of her life, no matter what happened.

Lily turned her thoughts to the excitement that lie ahead for her. Another part of Lily was anticipating what she hoped would turn out to be the most exciting new beginning in her life. Lily was restless. She felt that being almost seventeen years old now should qualify her as an adult and give her some independence.

She had spent her childhood being a very curious little girl and now that curiosity was besting her again. Her mother told her that this must all come from her father. The curious nature was manifested in wanting to fly from the cliffs in Forgotten Cove some days. When Lily was seven years old she told her mother that she wanted to "get inside" a neighbour to teach her to be kinder to the children that wanted to play hide and seek in her garden. Lily was hoping that her new cousins had similar curiosities about life.

As the huge Airbus floated through the night sky nearing the country and the city where the villa stood Lily felt a further awakening. It was a keen awareness of some of the passengers on the flight. As she looked at one woman, she could feel the woman's loneliness begin to envelop her. To Lily, she felt it was necessary to layer into this woman's mind to see what caused this loneliness. She stared at her, sensing this woman's dream to stay on vacation forever in New York City. The woman was being eaten up with her inability to have children and the fear that her husband would find a new wife because of this. It was simple to enter this mind that needed fulfillment in her life. Lily sat on her sill and dreamed of happy days as a child playing in the park without the cares and responsibilities of an adult. Lily next made the woman aware of the tiny life growing inside of her. She pulled back in time to see a playful smile grace the woman's face. To Lily it made sense for someone to be childlike and playful if they wanted to keep the attention of an adult. This would help the woman to remain calm enough to bring her child into the world.

Later, during the long flight Lily looked across the aisle at a young boy who appeared to carry the weight of the world upon his shoulders. When she layered him she found that he had been to a New York doctor. She could feel the illness inside of him which would eventually claim his life. He looked back at her and nodded as if to confirm this. She layered deeper to show him that the cosmos carried a promise to him that he would always remain a child. He would meet many other children who also would remain as he would in the innocent state forever. Lily felt today that she was seeing what existed in their recent memory without ever having to layer too deeply. It was exciting but frightening at the same time.

Much later a jolt awakened Lily when her mother touched her hands as the huge aircraft touched down, roughly bumping many times along the runway. They had dosed for a few hours and awoke to people excitedly grabbing bags filled with their goods from stores, such as Macy's, out of the overhead storage. Mother told her that someone from the villa was to meet them and escort them through the airport.

From this moment onward, Lily began to feel that she had truly left Forgotten Cove and her childhood behind. Today the rest of her life would begin. She quickly hugged her mother and let go her last childhood giggle.

15

The ride in the sleek silver limousine from the airport to the villa was exciting for Lily. She felt like a celebrity with the family crests of Olympus adorning the flags waving from two antennas and of course the conveniently darkened windows. She saw a harbor filled with boats of all sizes come into view. These boats were not boats but yachts never seen in Forgotten Cove. Lily had read about the wealth in this oil rich country but never could have imagined so many yachts in one small harbor.

The limo turned to climb a gentle slope in the otherwise flat landscape. The streets were very wide in this area made up of wealthy estates. Wrought iron gates guarded every estate they traveled past. Finally arriving, automatic gates slowly rolled open. The gates opened to a tropical paradise that would become her home for the next year. Lily gasped as they entered the Zeus villa. The driveway was endless. Gardens were filled with flowers and vines Lily had only seen in green houses. Palm trees filled the landscape. A stone mansion of epic proportions filled her view. It was as if the ancient Greece of history books were transported to this location.

Statuary of Greek gods filled the gardens closer to the house. As the car finally came to a stop, the house door opened and a lone dark haired woman stepped out to greet them. She introduced herself as Arabella to Lily, then turned and hugged Hannah, telling her it was so wonderful they should meet again.

Arabella and her mother chatted non-stop as they were escorted to adjoining bedrooms with their own private baths. They were told to rest as long as they needed in order to feel refreshed. Food and drink would be served to them in the bedroom suites until the following morning. By the next day Lily was eagerly waiting to meet the others that were closer to her in age.

Qamar and Ikram were a delight. The two were so much the same as Lily it felt as if they were both her sisters. Qamar was the daughter of Arabella and her father was Hermes too. Qamar, a natural beauty was tiny framed like Lily but had Arabella's deep brown eyes with thick black lashes. Her olive skinned face was the sculpture of every Greek goddess Lily had ever seen. Qamar was very unpretentious. Lily loved Qamar's shy smile that made her blush and look away every time she smiled. Ikram was the daughter of Aglaope who was the daughter of Melpomene. She was like her mother Aglaope in turn who was like her mother Melpomene and so they all bore a close resemblance to each other.

After spending a few hours of getting to know each other in the garden Lily felt as if she had spent her whole life with the two of them. It seemed the three were of one mind. They completed each others sentences and giggled every time it happened. It was wondrous how the three were raised in such different parts of the world but behaved as sisters.

Lily met the family matriarch, Mnemosyne upon her arrival at breakfast mid morning. She told the girls they all reminded her of her own nine daughters growing up in Greece. Lily felt so much at

the VILLA

home as if she had always known Qamar and Ikram. They thought alike, right down to the choices they made for their meals. Lily began to feel she had become more complete as a person since her arrival. When she was with them she felt more confident in her abilities as a half mortal person. Mel had been right about her fitting into the family. It was going to be a great holiday for a whole year. Lily felt like it was Christmas every morning that first week when she awoke in the beautiful mahogany bed covered in silks and furs. She was surprised when she first saw the furs as part of the bedding. She soon learned they were necessary because someone kept the air conditioning turned to a very cool temperature.

The three girls were presented with medieval style hand sewn abayas or robes with cowled hoods from Hermes. The abayas were made of the finest crepe de chine from China, hand stitched with golden coloured silk threads. The abayas were daintily buttoned with tiny black seashells imported from South Africa. These abayas flowed away from their body into an A-line to disguise the shape of their youthful bodies. Hermes had personally overseen to the designing and fabric of the robes. He traveled to Dubai himself and met with the world famous designer Thurayah. Hermes had given these gifts to each of the girls. Plus they each received an additional complete Thurayah wardrobe suitable for their young adult age. Thurayah was the top designer in her field for this generation's style of clothing worn in this part of the world. These robes would make them totally anonymous in Jeddah. Hermes wanted the girls to blend in with the local people so they could roam the city shops at will. Lily spent hours trying on each different outfit. She felt so exotic. The clothing was definitely glamorous and Lily felt very much a young glamorous woman while wearing the beautiful robes. Arabella and Qamar showed her how to apply her make-up so she resembled an exotic Arabian princess. This was exciting for Lily since she never had worn make-up in Forgotten Cove. She laughed as her mother chided Arabella for teaching Lily and her own daughter to look so exotic when they were supposed to remain unnoticed.

Hermes had decided that his son, Saon was responsible enough to oversee lessons for the girls in proper etiquette for their new lifestyle. Saon was a responsible person and had expressed an interest in meeting Ikram to his father for years now. Saon lived in the modern world. He did not show an interest in the lifestyle of the immortals. He spent his days and nights with his friend Chrys on a yacht moored in the Jeddah harbor.

The girls spent the balance of the first week getting to know each other, discovering their sameness. The three knew they were brought here to the villa to learn new skills and hone what skills they already had. Two weeks after letting the girls rest, Hermes had requested Melpomene and her daughters, her sisters Calliope and Thalia to be present for an important meeting with their mother Mnemosyne. The girls were invited to be present too. The meeting was to become a weekly progress report from Saon to his elders.

Lily, Ikram and Qamar had been escorted on many short journeys throughout the region in the following weeks. Hermes son and their escort, Saon was to care for their safety as instructed by Hermes. He was the son of Hermes and the immortal fountain nymph, Rhene. He was a little smaller in stature than his father but was as handsome as Hermes if not more handsome. Saon had flashing grey eyes with sand coloured hair that contrasted his deeply tanned skin.

Saon showed the three girls all he had learned from Hermes about layering. They understood what had been shown to them and practiced in the gardens daily using each other to layer. At first it was awkward for the girls. Growing up Lily experienced the episodes of knowing what others were thinking and feeling but never to the degree that she could communicate with a person's thoughts without them being aware. Practicing on each other had limits for the girls. They were aware that someone was wanting inside their mind and so agreed to become willing for each other. This also taught them to guard their thoughts.

Lily had never encountered such peaceful beauty as these well-tended gardens. Through a labyrinth of sprinklers, areas of the garden resembled a rain forest. Twice in a day while walking in the garden she encountered a pair of ocelots as tame as any house cat. These ocelots were imported a great distance from the jungles of South America. There were so many beautiful and exotic birds that Lily had only seen in books before seeing this garden. All of this was so new for Lily. She spent private time singing to the wildlife in the garden. It was a very peaceful spot. Some of the animals would stop close to her and listen. When Lily felt she had gained the trust of an animal she would layer into them. The garden animals were very unsettling to layer for her. She found that animals in a captive state were always on high alert trying not to leave any sill for her to enter. She had to gain a lot of trust from them. The female ocelot was first to trust her. Lily entered by the open sill into a world filled with memories of the huge canopy of trees blotting out the bright sun. The vegetation of the forest floor smelled a rich earthy smell. The ground was soft under the pads on her huge feet. Leaves caressed her as she skulked along the floor of the jungle. Lily pulled back to see tears in the ocelot's eyes. The ocelot communicated a primal longing for its freedom to her. Lily pulled out and run her fingers through the warm neck hair on the beautiful ocelot feeling it's loneliness for his far away home.

16

After a tour of the old part of the city one day, Saon took the girls to a super yacht moored in the Jeddah harbor to end the afternoon outing. The Jeddah harbor was filled with a least a dozen super sized yachts. This particular super yacht was obviously a sanctuary for young people living in the area. Saon introduced the girls to Chrysaor, the owner who chose to be called just Chrys. He was a descendant of what was called the Gorgon line or the children of Ceto and Phorcys. Chrys's family ancestors were neighbours of Mnemosyne and Zeus on Mount Olympus.

THE CHILDREN OF ZEUS HAD always roamed the hills of Olympus as young children with the children from Chrys's ancestral family. According to Saon, Chrys was someone they could trust as a good friend. Saon told the girls that Chrys and the younger immortals were not always in agreement with some of the old ways of the secretive immortals. They chose to enjoy the modern world just as it was at this time and to live in the moment.

Chrys was so handsome with dark flashing eyes. This was noticed immediately by all three girls. His shoulder length black wavy hair sparkled in the sunlight and Lily wanted to reach out to touch it. When he stood close to her she felt the magnetic pull toward him. Up close she stole a glance at the sea blue flecks of light in his eyes. Lily giggled with Qamar and Ikram on the trip back to the villa after the first meeting. The three felt quite comfortable around Saon and Chrys. Trust was being built with the decisions Saon made for them. All three felt this yacht would be the destination they would beg Saon to take them again.

The harbor lights of Jeddah twinkled like diamonds in the deep mauve backdrop of the western sky. It was immediately cooler with the ferocity of the sun's heat gone from sight. The last echoes of prayer from the mosques had ended and a quiet seeped across the land. The absence of people in the streets was common at this time of the evening. People were at home with their families. Chrys stared at the sky watching the stars blink on. Their tiny golden lights appeared one at a time as the sky deepened from the mauve color into the deepest purple. He felt content. A tiny breeze carried the scent of Arabia to his yacht. He thought about his new friends Qamar, Ikram and Lily, especially Lily. Chrys knew they were the same as him. They were descendent of an immortal. Chrys came from long line of very proud people who called Mount Olympus home. He had been visiting his family on Olympus since he was a young boy. Chrys thought of Phorcys and Ceto to be as grandparent figures to him. He was very much favored by them because of his uncanny resemblance to his ancestor also with the name Chrysaor. Chrys had been named for him. The original Chrysaor was one of the sons of Medusa, the favored daughter of Phorcys and Ceto. Medusa, their beloved daughter was brutally raped by Poseidon as a young girl, and then she was punished by Athena as if she had caused this attention to herself by Poseidon. Through a series of events the mighty Zeus ordered that the monster Medusa had become, as result of the curse from Athena, must be destroyed.

Ceto had never spent a day in her life that she did not mourn Medusa. This is why Ceto passed tales of Medusa to descendents of her daughter. She kept Medusa's memory alive in her family. This was also the reason she favored Chrys. Chrys had inherited the even-tempered ways and the tranquil personality of Ceto's beloved Medusa. Whenever Ceto spent happy times with Chrys the painful memories of her loss would be relived afterward for days. The wound had never healed for her. Ceto spent her life missing the daughter who made her so happy. Ceto felt as if Chrys filled part of that void for her. He gave Ceto temporary release from the raw pain caused by the loss of her much cherished daughter, Medusa.

Chrys had decided long ago as a small boy that he would learn to dive to collect the coral from the Red Sea that meant so much to Ceto. He would do this as a gesture of kindness toward Ceto. The specific coral he was looking for was a red coral. It was not the red coral found in many deposits in reefs around the world. It was blood red coral, the deep garnet color of blood. It came from the drops of blood that fell from the head of Medusa into the sea as Perseus flew over the Red Sea. Perseus flew over the sea carrying the head of Medusa to Zeus who was in residence at the Jeddah villa waiting for the confirmation of her death from Perseus. As the god of Olympus it was Zeus who decided the final fate of Medusa. Ceto felt this collection of red coral may give her some closure in dealing with the immense loss of her beloved Medusa. It would bring at least part of some remaining pieces of her child back to her mother.

the VILLA

Chrys spent many millions of dollars on a lifestyle and a yacht where he would live. This would be his home. Chrys had decided to name his yacht, "Garnet". He sailed the Garnet from the Mediterranean Sea where it was purchased into the Red Sea and down the coast. Chrys moored his floating home in the Jeddah harbor. It was here Chrys decided to make his permanent home. Chrys hired the local people to spend time diving with him, teaching him about the under water landscape and the underwater caves. Throughout the years Chrys became an expert diving instructor. He learned from an expert teaching instructor who taught him well. Chrys learned about the types of coral along the coasts of the Red Sea from the local university. Divers came in from all areas of the world to dive in the reefs here. The yacht gained a reputation through the years as a place where a lot the young people gathered. This was where Saon first met and become a close friend of Chrys. The two dived together throughout the years, harvesting the red coral. Chrys never divulged to Saon the reason he collected red coral. It was unspoken. Saon decided the reason must be for the drops of Medusa's blood. This was Chrys private matter and Chrys would share it someday when he felt it was okay to do so with Saon.

17

Finally an evening more close to two months after arriving, Lily would meet privately with her father Hermes. All who were present at the villa would meet with Hermes privately before they attended the weekly meeting. Afterward Hermes would meet again with the attendees to be sure everyone understood their responsibility to the new half mortals. Hermes talked to Lily of responsibility to the family and the history of Zeus on Olympus. Hermes professed his love for her mother. Lily questioned this.

Lily spoke meekly, "Father, how can you love my mother, Arabella and Rhene at the same time? I am sure if it is the same situation as the other Zeus families then there are many others you have too." Hermes let out a great laugh. "You are truly my daughter. Lily, you are young. I come from a time when thought was much different about these things. For now Lily you will have to just trust me that I do love your mother. I want you to know you can come to me whenever you need to talk or understand something. Now you join Qamar and Ikram and meet in the great room with the others."

the VILLA

When the girls entered the great room for the meeting later, Hermes and Mnemosyne were deep in conversation. Hermes acknowledged each of them separately then began to speak, directing his conversation toward the three youngest members of the family in the room.

"The three of you have learned your crafts quite easily this past while from Saon but none of you have been tested for your skills against your own will.

Some of you have had the opportunity and learned from Melpomene as Qamar and Lily have or learned from your own mother as Ikram has done. We often compare our lives to a cloth fabric. There are many folds and layers in such a piece of fabric. In between these layers and folds are lives. In these lives are again many layers of consciousness. We gods or immortals as we prefer to call ourselves can enter into these layers. We can live in the different layers of consciousness in a persons mind, in their world, in a mind other than our own. We can also enter another beings consciousness. The layer in which we inhabit and control can become filled with some of our knowledge if we choose. This is why you are here. It is important that the information layered into your mind is from Zeus family members and is in keeping with Zeus ideals. We can read the thoughts of each other in our family and others outside Zeus family although we can not read them as well as a family member. Where we want to be of service to a person, we become of service to that person. Mel helped your mother to retrieve her husband's soul by layering her, Lily. I spoke with Mnemosyne and her daughters about this. Mnemosyne agrees that Hannah had a destiny in life that would bring her into our family life.

With all of this said there is one important concept of layering you must come to know and understand. You must learn that you must be on high alert at all times. Two of you young ladies, Qamar and Lily are born of an immortal father and a human mother. This means you are a half mortal. Ikram, Agloapes's daughter is born of an immortal mother but not an immortal father. He was also human. Ikram is also a half mortal. The meaning of all of this is that you are not entirely immortal. You must guard this lack of immortality since it can be taken from you by an immortal being. You possess what we immortals possess as powers but all of us possess our powers in varying degrees. The powers are skills we must sharpen or they may not serve you as well as you need them to serve when you summon them. The muses and their mother will help you with proficiency. It is very important to hone these skills as a well-sharpened blade to be ready for anything."

Hermes paused before continuing, "I need to share something further of a very serious nature with all of you. The reason you were invited to the villa is to address the unrest happening on the island of the Gorgons.

Years ago Melpomene befriended your mother, Lily. The reason was because of Mel's daughter Aglaope causing the death of your mother's husband. She stole his soul. Aglaope gave this soul to Persephone who wanted to own it as well as many others out of her greedy nature. Melpomene and Calliope designed a plan to trade Persephone his soul for one hundred souls that were previously captured by Medusa who was the most powerful of the Gorgon sisters. They completed this plan and laid Jack Gallegars soul to rest.

Years earlier in a different event Medusa decided to attack the Muses to repay Zeus for what she thought was his part in her violation at the temple. Zeus heard of this so he sent Perseus to slay Medusa. Medusa was only one of three sisters living on this island at the time. She also was the only half mortal of her sisters, the same as you three ladies. The other sisters were immortals. Perseus beheaded her and gave Medusa's head to Zeus as a trophy and that is where it is thought to still remain throughout all time.

When we went to take the hundred souls from the island of the Gorgons a little over sixteen years ago to honor the trade for Jack Gallegar's soul, it seems we disturbed the immortal sisters of Medusa. A few months ago I found something pinned to the gate of the underworld on the Island of Anthemoessa. It was a note and is the main reason you have been summoned. Mnemosyne and I have been given authority by Zeus to handle the situation. I will read the note to you."

Hermes drew a piece of parchment from inside his vest and read it to the others in the room.

HE CONTINUED, "BECAUSE YOU WERE part of the group who stole the captured souls belonging to Medusa, you must make payment. We will take captive all of your half mortal descendents souls born into the Zeus family. We will imprison them on the island of the Gorgons until the hundred souls have been returned to the island of the Gorgons. We will strike a bargain for such possessions."

Grave unbroken silence filled the room. Fear gripped Hannah. She reached for the hand of her beloved daughter, her reason for life. She felt an arm around her shoulder. Numbly she turned to face Arabella. Melpomene caught this interaction and spoke first.

"Wait, Hermes, what is meant by a bargain for these possessions?"

"Let me finish Mel. I have spoken with the two immortal Gorgon sisters. They have agreed that we can try to get these souls back from Persephone. That is the reason why you are here, Calli. I need you to persuade Persephone of this. Otherwise our alternative is that we must guard our half mortals daily, forever."

Melpomene spoke first after listening to what Hermes told them. It seemed Arabella and Hannah couldn't find words to express the thoughts forming in their mind. Mel reached out to hold Hannah's free hand while she spoke.

"Hannah, I will guard Lily as I would my own daughters. I am confident that we will resolve this without anyone being hurt. Calli and I will travel to Olympus and speak with the family of Medusa to ensure this."

From across the room Aglaope listened. She could see the easiness of the interaction between her mother and Hannah. It was the bond she had never experienced with her mother. This was the single biggest reason Aglaope always felt anger toward her mother. What of Ikram? Would her mother ensure her safety too? Aglaope carefully curbed her rising need to let loose her sirens wail on the room. Aglaope was a powerful siren but slowed her thoughts when she noticed her grandmother Mnemosyne, the great matriarch of the family watching her reaction to all of this. Her grandmother was the one person she would never challenge.

Mnemosyne spoke first before anyone else could. "Melpomene, you must be responsible for all three of the girl's safety. Your own granddaughter, Ikram and daughter Aglaope need to be afforded every consideration right now. Aglaope and Ikram live in isolation on the island of flowers. Their absolute safety must be addressed. Hermes and I will speak with Zeus for a further resolution."

Directing the conversation toward the three girls and Hannah, Mnemosyne went on, "Years ago Phorcys and Ceto were our closest friends and neighbours on Olympus. After the nightmare of what happened to Medusa at such a young age they rarely have spoken again with us. I realize it has been centuries since this incident happened but Ceto has always felt that Zeus should never have sent

Perseus to stop the madness that Athena inflicted on Medusa. It was truly a tragedy."

"*Yes,*" Melpomene thought silently, "*it was this very tragedy that shaped my life.*" Her thoughts steeped in the overwhelming sadness began to take over again. The heaviness of the loss of her daughters made tears spring suddenly to her eyes.

Aglaope stared at her mother dabbing her tears as Mel gave her an apology. Mel assured Aglaope that her own granddaughter Ikram would be her greatest priority. Aglaope did feel a little uneasy with Ikram and her being so isolated on Anthemoessa. Ikram loved the island and refused all offers to live anywhere else on earth. This was home. The island was where she had always wanted to stay forever. Through the years Aglaope had many young animals brought to the island as playmates for Ikram. Aglaope was aware that her mother had always felt that Ikram was more like her own daughter than any of her own three daughters had ever been. Her own daughters were like their father Achelous. Ikram was not headstrong or challenging like her mother. Ikrams physical appearance obviously came from her oriental father. She was a raven haired beauty since birth with very pale porcelain skin. Ikram was a small framed girl much the same as the sailor who was her father from the orient. The sailor, her father, whose last mistake on earth was to follow the sound when he heard Aglaope singing as he passed the island years before. Ikram had his dark eyes that were almond shaped but carried the sadness of the world in them as her grandmother Melpomene did. Ikram spent her childhood roaming the fields of beautiful flowers. She loved the earth for the way it smelled and for what it gave to her. While lazing in the sun with the wolves her mother brought to the island, Ikram would sing gently as they would close their eyes in complete trust of this human just as her grandmother Melpomene had done as a child. Sometimes her mother would take her to Olympus. She decided if she were to ever leave the island it would be to live on Olympus to roam the beautiful peaks and meadows. Some of time while Ikram was growing up was spent at the home of her maternal grandfather, Achelous. Ikram was a little afraid of this gruff man. When she stared at him she saw horns and hooves. He ruled the river with an iron fist. Achelous kingdom was where her mother lived as a child. Ikram knew her mother was sent away to the beautiful island of flowers as a punishment. Ikram felt that this would not have been considered punishment for her to be away from that river. There were too many people living there. That was what Achelous wanted. He wanted to hide his despair for the loss of his daughters. He did not want to ever be alone. Achelous wanted to have many people around him at all times. He blamed Melpomene for his daughters being sirens. Mel did not keep absolute control at all times over the girls. Achelous felt this was the reason Persephone was kidnapped and the reason he was alone.

Ikram shared the disposition of great sadness with her grandmother Melpomene. She loved walking high on Olympus with Mel telling her childhood tales from Olympus. Ikram loved the rare occasions when Mel would stay on the island with her and her mother. Mel taught Ikram how to make glorious wreaths from the flowers to wear as a natural crown by weaving the flowers with ribbons and long grasses. Ikram would always remember the days of running through the meadows on the island crowned with flowers trailing behind her in long tails, scattering petals from all of the other flowers. These were happy times. She felt so free with the flowered garlands streaming behind her, young wolves and fox at her feet trying to keep up with the fleet footed Ikram. Ikram never ventured near to the gate to the underworld on Anthemoessa or the gate on the river when they visited her fathers home on the Achelous River. Aglaope had warned her of the danger and Ikram was an obedient child. To Ikram, it was a stressful time being on the Achelous River just in knowing what happened to her mother and aunts as children growing up there. The abrupt loss of innocence her mother endured was not different to her than the loss of innocence that Medusa and Persephone experienced as children.

Hermes laughed at a remark being passed on to him by Calli. This brought everyone back into the room and away from their own private thoughts.

The three girls looked at each other with unspoken intent. It was obvious to Calli they did not feel as afraid as they should of this threat scrawled on parchment and left pinned to the gates of the underworld. Their plan was to have Saon escort them back to the beautiful yacht moored in the harbor as soon as this meeting would end. More than one of them wanted to look deeply into the eyes of Chrysaor. Lily thought of how she had more than just a mild schoolgirl crush on him and how embarrassed she would feel if he rejected her. Lily was not so innocent that she could not see the same kind of attraction between Saon and Ikram. She noticed they seemed to only have eyes for each other. Lily brushed aside any fear she felt from the information conveyed by Hermes. She hoped the others had also done this and would still plan to visit the yacht tonight.

Lily looked at Hermes again. Hermes was telling the group of the plan to visit Olympus with Calli to convince Phorcys and Ceto to aid him in talking with Medusa's sisters. The plan was to ensure the safety of the half mortals and to convince Persephone to return at least some souls to the island of the Gorgons. With this he wrapped up the meeting.

Hermes looked at Saon sternly. "Saon, I want you to never leave the side of these three girls. Never trust anyone with them alone. Do you understand?" Saon nodded his head in the affirmative.

18

Saon spoke in hushed tones when he told the three girls they would join Chrys that evening with him. They would wait until the others had settled for the night and meet by the fountain in the back garden. Saon instructed them to dress for a party. This brought about giggles of happiness as the three wore their fanciest looking hooded abaya to cover the summer-like outfits they had purchased at a designer shop in downtown Jeddah while touring the city. Lily felt that spending Saon's money was easier than asking her mother for some of the small amount of cash they brought with them. Ikram and Qamar were deep in conversation about Ikram's romantic interest in Saon as they were busy touching up their make-up and hair. They had both confided to Lily earlier that they did not have the benefit she had in going to school with other girls and boys the same age as they were. They had never shared giggles over boys with a sister and this was exciting for them to do now. Secret dreams of the young girls were carefully guarded and kept away from all-knowing parents. As she entered the end of her young teen years, Lily had longed for a best friend. This was answered

the VILLA

doubly, for now she had two others who were as sisters to her, two that understood her half mortal life and how she differed from all of her school friends. Lily was excited about attending her first real party and maybe just a little more excited to see Chrys again.

When the three were prepared for the party and each had checked the halls outsides their mother's bedroom for activity, they slipped out to the back garden gate to meet with Saon. During the walk down the slope toward the harbor and Chrys's yacht, Saon told them they were going to Tangier to a party.

Qamar stopped short in her tracks. "Tangier! That is in another country, another continent! Saon, do you realize how far away that is for the three of us?"

"Wait, Qamar," Saon replied, "Chrys will support you and Lily for the quick flight. He is strong so by letting both of you use him for support in case you lose focus or tire from the journey, we should be okay. I will do the same for Ikram. Both Chrys and I have wanted to go to one of Zharah's parties for a long while. Zharah is related to Chrys. Her parties are famous throughout the Mediterranean Riviera. Zharah's affairs attract the trendy crowd and a lot of fun people. I think we deserve this bit of this fun since we have been working so hard on our training this past while."

They all looked at each other and laughed while nodding in agreement.

The excitement was high as Chrys met the four on deck. Chrys relieved Saon by taking charge of Lily and Qamar, the two girls leaving Saon alone with Ikram for awhile. Instructions were given to Lily and Qamar to hold tight to Chrys while in flight in case they tire. The girls were going to fast travel to Tangier.

"Tangier! You did say all the way to Tangier, Chrys." Qamar's eyes were huge as she anticipated the journey.

"Yes, Tangier," Chrys laughed at Qamar, "my cousin Zharah will have a party tonight. This is a great opportunity for you ladies to meet some of the younger immortals and half mortals. What do you say, Lily?"

Lily answered, unable to keep eye contact with Chrys for more than a few seconds a one time. "I read a lot about Tangier in school but never thought I would ever be going there. I feel excited." I am smitten she giggled to herself. Chrys flashed a smile that told her he was too.

They talked excitedly about staying close together at the party and watching out for each other. In the next few minutes the three held hands making the circle complete as they watched Ikram and Saon do the same thus enabling the five travelers to reach Morocco in mere minutes. The fast travel wasn't any different than closing your eyes on a fast moving escalator for the half mortals.

Lily could immediately feel the pulsing vibrancy in the narrow streets of old Tangier. Music and excited conversations were in progress in every direction she looked. Lily looked down upon these narrow streets filled with covered passages into shops and homes. Even before they alit outside a very large villa set atop the rocky cliffs the pulsing music from inside could be heard. At the villa the views of the Atlantic were breathtaking. The treacherous coastline guarded walled courtyards protecting the many villas built into the cliffs. Did this mean she was really learning to accept her new life without question? The fleeting thought entered Lily's mind when she glanced toward the waves breaking on the rocks below. It reminded her of Forgotten Cove. Lily thought to herself of the excitement of being so far from the villa with people she did not even know for more than two months. Here she was thousands of miles from home attending a function unlike any function she had ever dreamed of in Forgotten Cove.

the VILLA

The European influenced architecture of the villa was set in an Andalusian style garden, mixing the flowers with the vegetables. This home was a dwarf compared to the Jeddah villa but was still huge compared to the other villas in the area. Tangier was a noisy city unlike the quiet of Jeddah. People filled the streets laughing, talking and partying even at this late hour. Chrys mentioned to Lily that the young Moroccans used the caves in the sides of the hills for parties. The excitement filled Lily as she breathed the aromatic ocean breezes blowing toward the Atlas Mountains.

LILY STARED AROUND THE HALF darkened room as she entered wanting to inhale into her memory all she saw tonight. She noticed the large number of full-sized human like statues in the room. They were so realistic that Lily could hardly see a difference in them and the people in the darkened room. Ikram and Saon moved off quickly to a darkened corner, Lily assumed they wanted to be alone. Qamar tugged at her sleeve to slow down but Lily ignored her, she was trying to keep stride with Chrys. Chrys had acknowledged a group of people on the far side of the room. As they approached the group Lily's eyes were drawn to a younger lady who appeared to be close to her age. She was surrounded by a pulsing aura of a deep purple colour. In this world Lily had learned that a person is not always what they appear. Appearances may be very much what the viewer wants to see in the normal world but in the world of the immortals, appearances are what the half mortal or immortal wants others to see of them.

"Zharah," Chrys began, "I want you to meet my new friends Qamar and Lily. They live at the Zeus Villa in Jeddah." To Lily and Qamar, Chrys related that Zharah was in the same family and they were both descendant of Medusa. When Chrys mentioned Medusa, Lily saw a spark, almost like lightning appear momentarily in Zharah's eyes. Zharah was very beautiful, very exotic looking and her words were spoken softly like a gentle rain falling, welcoming the two young ladies. She told them to mingle and enjoy the night. She went on to tell them her door was open to them at any time. Lily felt a strong pull from Zharah. Zharah was not looking at or speaking aloud to Lily when Lily felt her communicate her future bonds with her. Lily stared at the back of Zharah's head when she turned to cross the room.

In a flash Zharah turned around to face her and spoke aloud to Lily, "You are right about being drawn to me, Lily, we are as sisters. One day you will own the heart of Chrysaor." These words struck Lily like a lightning bolt. Zharah could see this and laughed. Lily felt a moment of confusion. She continued, "Lily you are still a baby in this world, you have much to learn. I will be here to teach you. Be patient and enjoy learning about this world," Zharah smiled at Lily. This surprised and embarrassed Lily to have her name linked to Chrys when she barely knew him. As the evening progressed Lily started to feel a little more at ease. The music, food and drinks were in great supply.

Halfway throughout the evening Qamar became increasingly aware of a small group of people watching her and Lily. Several times she saw them talking with Zharah. They were all watching her and Lily mingle with the guests from the Spanish mainland. Qamar noticed that the group were dressed in hooded long drab robes making it impossible to know if they were male or female. It was definitely not party attire. Qamar noticed them mainly because of their large size. She mentioned this to Lily who only had eyes for Chrys and would not have noticed if the floor fell out from under them. Qamar could see that Lily was bedazzled by Chrys. She didn't have to tell Qamar of her interest in him. Chrys answered her query. He told Qamar this small group lived somewhere on the Mediterranean and told Qamar further to stay away from them. They turned up sometimes at Zharah's parties. That would not be a problem for Qamar as they made her feel more than a bit of discomfort. Qamar was sure it would not be a problem for Lily since the only person in her world was Chrys at the moment. Seeing that Lily and Chrys had eyes only for each other, Qamar decided against asking Chrys about the life size statues that filled the room. It seemed in the darkened room the eyes of a few of the statues moved or appeared to move. Qamar decided it was a trick of the low lighting so refocused her thoughts on the other people at the party.

Tonight was a night that set the pace for the next eight months. Chrys entertained on his yacht. Zharah entertained at the villa in Tangier. Saon taught the girls how to become an adept in sensory perceptions and communication without words. Each of the girls learned to become the travel companion of an immortal. Ikram and Saon seemed to have put their romance on a fast track. Saon had learned quite well how to please Aglaope. Ikram accepted an invitation for her and her mother to join Saon on a trip to Samothrace, his island, his home. They would go for a couple of months. This prompted Lily to find better ways to entice Qamar into accompanying her late at night to Chrys's yacht. Lily felt she could never wait for Saon and Ikram to return and escort them.

Chrys was aware Saon and Ikram would be visiting his home on Samothrace Island. Lily and Qamar continued to visit the yacht in the small hours of the night for the next two months.

19

Late one evening, close to the end of the second month and impatiently waiting for Saon and Ikram to return, Lily crept through the halls of the villa to Qamar's quarters. She could hear someone talking in the sleeping suites. Lily crept closer and saw Arabella, Qamar's mother in her rooms. Lily waited for an hour and checked again. Arabella was still talking with Qamar in her bedroom. She thought of not seeing Chrys that night then quickly decided she would go alone to the yacht. Lily returned to her room after checking if her mother was asleep, carefully dressed fully in her robes and went out through the back garden gate, down the gentle slope to the harbor. She felt a little fear of what would happen to her if she got caught by the guards from the villa but stifled the thought knowing it was only a fifteen minute run.

As Lily neared the yacht a small group of hooded people heading in the same direction as she was walking stopped her. They questioned her as to where she was going at this hour. Then in the next moment one of them said to her, "You are one of the new half mortals from the Zeus villa".

Lily wanted to deny this with an elaborate explanation she was preparing but before she could speak they threw a huge cloak over her head and stifled any attempt of her screaming for help. Darkness followed quickly as Lily inhaled the chemical that put her into a deep sleep.

What she thought had to be hours later, Lily struggled back through the layers of consciousness. The unfamiliar chemical smell became apparent again as she removed the sack like cloak covering her head. Lily looked around, trying to assess her surroundings. As she recognized the sounds that came from above her along with the movement to be the sounds of a motorized boat moving across water. Lily realized that she was in a confined storage space inside of a type of wooden container. Lily began to think she was being kidnapped. The faces of the three people she saw before ending up here on this boat were beginning to come back to her. They were hideous. More than one of them appeared to only have one eye. They looked similar to the old crones in fairy tales her mother read her as a child. She thought they may have appeared to look this way because she was drugged. The air still smelled of the chemical that made her lose consciousness. Lily started to panic as she fully realized that she did see how frightening the kidnappers looked before she was drugged. It could have been masks.

"Oh no, now I have really made a mess!" Lily spoke aloud then quickly stifled her voice in case somebody was around waiting for her to wake up. She had thought of what everyone at the villa was going to say and especially of her mother's panic when they realized she was not in her room. Lily hoped they would see she was not anywhere on the villa site and begin to look for her soon. Chris would tell them she never made it to his yacht last evening. Qamar would show them the path they always took to get to the yacht. This is what Lily hoped would happen soon. Someone would find her.

Someone had to be looking for her. She felt uncomfortable in the confined space that reeked of chemicals. Lily did not dare to think of what was happening. Thoughts of being kidnapped and perhaps being sold to some seedy human slave market were nagging at her to give them life. It was difficult for her to know how long she had been unconscious. Her legs and arms ached from the cramped position she was forced into while unconscious inside the wooden trunk.

The chemical smell was giving her a headache. It made her feel a little dizzy. She had to find a way to move toward some fresher air. Lily pushed at the sides of the container. It moved easily. She climbed out of what was an oversized trunk and lowered the lid very quietly with a slow movement so as not to alert anyone in the area. She looked around and realized she was in the bottom of an older wooden boat with a ladder leading to the deck above. Lily knew she could climb the ladder and rush to jump overboard but also considered that she may be miles from any land. There would have to be a different way to escape. She sat down wedged in a space behind the trunk to think. Her head ached from the chemical smell somewhere close to her. Lily faded into unconsciousness once more, welcoming the small refuge.

Arms grabbed her and pulled her to her feet. Lily struggled awake. She screamed and tried to pull away from whoever the person was grabbing at her. She focused in the semi-dark on one of them. It was a crone, the crone of the fairy tales from childhood. Lily screamed again and tried to get away. There were at least two of them grabbing her, pulling her across the boat bottom. Wild thoughts were coming into her mind. Lily hoped she was dreaming. *It would end.* She would wake up at the villa. *This isn't happening.* Lily didn't know how long she had been unconscious in the bottom of the boat and hoped someone at the villa noticed she was missing.

Lily kept struggling, trying to resist them. They were strong and easily handled her. She was lifted into the open air. Lily could smell the sea as hands pushed her into what felt like an oversized bag. Again Lily was drugged as a cloth soaked in a chemical covered her face. Shortly after the agony began with what felt as if she were being dragged along the rocky ground Lily felt her consciousness begin to leave her. She welcomed the black again as she felt herself fade away from the horror of knowing her own fate.

20

This past week had been peaceful. In her memory Aglaope could not remember a time when she had looked forward to the sunrise every day. Aglaope felt closer to Ikram than any person ever in her life. She loved the island of Samothrace. It was a beautiful island that reminded her of growing up near the River Achelous. The weeks passed with many banquets and much celebrating by the locals with the official engagement of Saon to her only child. Aglaope found that the family of Saon welcomed her as much as they welcomed Ikram. They treated her as an honored woman. She trusted that a new beginning was about to take place in her life. Aglaope had never had night dreams as a child or as a woman but since she come to Samothrace, dreams of happy times in her life visited her every night. She prepared herself for a peaceful sleep knowing that it was now time to start preparing for the return to the villa with the happy news of her daughters wedding in the coming months. Aglaope drifted off into a peaceful sleep.

Somewhere lost in the undefined layer of childhood memories a little before dawn, Aglaope laughed aloud as she and her two sisters run across the field of flowers, scattering seeds and petals in every direction. All of Zeus family spent private summers at the idyllic family home of his daughter Melpomene and her husband Achelous. The sprawling villa was serenely nestled in the meadows in an area with the gentlest flow of the River Achelous. The three sisters run, laughing and squealing in pursuit of their visitor, Persephone, as she run through the field ahead of them, away from the safety of the flowers. Aglaope stirred in her sleep as she started to feel the little tug of fear. The children neared the edge of the gardens. Mother had warned them daily of the dangers of leaving the fields of flowers. She looked in the direction that Persephone raced to catch up with her. Aglaope wanted to encourage her to run back toward the villa. Ahead of Persephone a group of three large people covered up in cowled robes appeared from nowhere it seemed. They grabbed at Persephone as she kicked and screamed to escape from them. The three sisters, frightened, stopped dead in their tracks. The sun disappeared quickly as a bolt of lightning cracked open the newly blackened sky. The scene playing out in front of the sisters became surreal. It felt as if time and all sounds stopped. The wind kicked up dust into Aglaope's eyes. This slammed her back to the present and the reality of what was happening. She looked in the direction of where Persephone had run. Persephone was no longer in front of them. Aglaope screamed before turning to run with her sisters as if the devil were at their heels. Aglaope run straight home fearing this devil may know where she lived if he had seen her.

The dream brought Aglaope quickly awake with a need to vent her siren's song. She opened her eyes and tried to focus on the sleeping girl beside her, deeply immersed in her own dreams. Aglaope's mind came back to the present as she realized she had been dreaming of the day Persephone was taken. It had affected her childhood and then had poisoned the rest of her life. This was her dear daughter beside her. Ikram meant everything to Aglaope. If she were ever taken from her as Persephone was taken from Demeter, the pain would be unimaginable. A painful wail was rising from deep inside Aglaope as she stared out of the window at the rising sun. She felt firm hands grip her.

"Mother, wake up. You are beginning to wail". Aglaope heard Ikram whispering very loudly and stifled the wail. Ikram carried on, "You were having a nightmare and starting to scream. Did you forget where you are? We are guests at Saon's family villa. I didn't want them to hear you and come running into the room thinking we were being attacked."

Aglaope gathered her thoughts before she responded. "Ikram, I have told you of the event that happened to your aunts, Pisinoe, Thelxiepia and to me long before you were born. I could never remember as a child who took Demeter's daughter, Persephone. I couldn't even tell you if it were men or women or more than one person. I was so traumatized by that event, then even more by everything that happened to mother and father afterward. I become so filled with hate, blaming your grandmother for everything in my life. I was so filled with vengeance that I did not give too much thought to anything except revenge upon the world for my fate. Now everything has changed. I have you and soon we may have Saon come into our family. She playfully teased Ikram. I am a happier person now. Last night I was dreaming of the day Persephone was taken and for the first time ever in my dream I saw that it was three people in cowled robes. They were like the grae ladies from Olympus that stole Persephone that day. It doesn't matter much now but it may mean that I am healing the hate I have for others inside my heart. I do see that my own mother must have been in hell without her daughters safely at home with her. I can feel this more now that I am a happier person."

the VILLA

There was a light tap on the door. Ikram and Aglaope were told breakfast was to be served in the garden. They prepared their selves for another day. Today they would meet with Saon's mother, Rhene for the last time to finalize the wedding ceremony. Saon's mother was away for last three weeks of their visit, but now had returned. She was anxious to meet them both again and discuss the betrothal of her son to Ikram. Saon's mother was a water nymph. Rhene was very delicate and also very beautiful, a true nymph. Aglaope had heard stories of Hermes chasing the water nymph he professed such a great love for. Rhene was the ruling nymph who lived on the island of Samothrace. She was also the guardian of the spring of fresh water, the source that fed the island.

Aglaope had heard many stories whispered about Hermes and his many loves. This story with Rhene was of a nymph that kept Hermes attention longer than any of Hermes other loves. This and the story of how he was continuously spurned by Persephone were by far the most interesting.

The island of Samothrace looked a lot like Anthemoessa. Herbs grew wild. This included oregano, thyme and St. John's Wort. Mint, lemon balm and chamomile filled the evening air. The island was protected by a towering majestic mountain in the north. It was fragrant with the smell of the flowers in every direction that Aglaope looked. She knew that the future of Ikram was here since Saon was in charge of the island together with his mother. Aglaope felt this meeting was for that purpose and was prepared for it. Everyone she met that day were naturally soft spoken and kind to her. Rhene was as concerned as she was about Saon and Ikram. The two mothers made a pact to give all the assistance needed for them to move forward in their new life together. Aglaope could see that Ikram was totally smitten by Saon. Ikram had decided to make the island her home on a part time basis at the invitation of Rhene. It felt like life was finally beginning to Aglaope. Tomorrow they would journey back to the villa in Jeddah. Aglaope was excited to tell everyone at the villa, even excited to tell her mother, the great muse of tragedy, how there may be hope for them to become closer as the family moves toward this new adventure together.

Aglaope stared at the star-studded inky black sky that night as she decided she would stay only one day at the villa in Jeddah before traveling back to her island of flowers with Ikram to prepare for the new direction their life was about to take. They would plan for a wedding in a meadow. For the first time since Ikram was born she felt a gentle peace descend upon her. Maybe this is the reason why she dreamed of Persephone's kidnapping and her own childhood. Aglaope brushed away the image of the three cowl robed people grabbing Persephone. This was supposed to be a happy time. She would not let anything interfere, not even thoughts of her unhappy childhood. It was time for her to believe there would be happiness in her future life.

21

A day later at the villa in Jeddah, the siren of the sea stifled another wail. She and Ikram were brought up to date on the current status with the missing Lily. Aglaope stared at Hannah who was definitely not in control of her emotions. Hannah sat still with her mouth slightly opened. Her eyes were unfocused, staring at some imagined horror that filled her mind. Part of Aglaope felt empathy toward Hannah who was also a mother and loved her daughter as much as Aglaope loved Ikram. Another part of Aglaope felt the presence of the memory of the jealousy she had come to feel with Hannah and her mother's relationship, something she had never shared with Mel. This and the thought that it may have been her daughter brought the wail of the siren close to the surface. She stifled it with great resolve and brought herself back to the moment. Ikram was aware of this and grasped her mother's hands tightly to get her attention. Aglaope's throat had swollen and her gills for water breathing had started to appear. Her eyes widened as she saw her beloved daughter in front of her willing her to fight off the wail. Aglaope struggled for the moment as it passed along with her melodious assault. The others in the room were too immersed in the present problem and its resolution to see the subtle changes in Aglaope.

A very concerned Hermes and Melpomene were deep in conversation with Arabella. They were carefully going over the details of Saon, Ikram, Lily and Qamar's nightly visits to the yacht. Hermes and Melpomene were aware of the parties on the yacht and even the trips to Tangier. They had decided to keep watch on the young members of the family with the use of the security guards following them until they reached their destination on the yacht safely every evening. Hermes knew he was taking a chance to trust the half mortals in Tangier but also knew that neither Chrys nor Saon would let them out of their sight for a moment of time.

Hermes sternly related to everyone in the room the dark side of his concerns.

"You three half mortals are aware of Chrys's background. You know why he has the yacht moored here instead of in any other spot on this earth. Even if he is completely reliable and trustworthy, the people around him may not be straight with their motives for being in his company. I need any information to follow up on, no matter how trivial it may appear. What can you tell me?"

Ikram opened up to Hermes first. "We have been night flying to Morocco and once to the south coast of the Mediterranean for parties. I remember Qamar telling me the discomfort she felt in Morocco with three hooded young men that she felt were stalking her at a party of Chrys's cousin."

Qamar piped in. "That's true but after a while they became interested in other guests. I couldn't see their faces because they were wearing cowled robes. I remember the first time I saw them talking with Zharah, I thought they were girls because I heard a feminine laugh from them. I remember too, being uneasy at people who looked very similar to them watching us as we boarded Chrys's yacht every night. They stayed in the shadows behind the pile of old fishing nets close to Chrys's yacht. I told myself that they were maybe someone watching over us from the villa, someone who followed us to the yacht."

Mel answered that. "Qamar, that is unreasonable. What would a pile of fishing nets be doing on a dock to moor yachts only? There are no fishing boats on that pier. We asked you to be careful. We had our reasons. You heard the contents of the note pinned to the gate on Anthemoessa." Qamar looked to Ikram for help. Ikram looked in her mother's direction as Aglaope touched Ikram in a gesture to allow her to speak.

Aglaope spoke. "I know I have not been so easy to get along with through the years but I would like to add something to this conversation that may be important. Ikram and I were the guests of Saons family this past while. I felt so rested and at ease on that island. I had a very disturbing night terror while I was at the villa on Samothrace. You see, ever since I was a child I have felt blame put on to me and on my sisters to do with the disappearance of Persephone." Aglaope stared into Mel's eyes as if to elicit a reaction and continued. "We were told that our parents did not hold us responsible but Demeter certainly did. I was only a child and felt very much traumatized. I closed my mind to the memory of that day, the memory that frightened me into silence. I blocked the memory surfacing with my wailing, my siren song. I closed my mind to whom or what I saw the day Persephone was taken. Up until I was at Saon's family villa in such a relaxed state I kept it locked from my conscious memory. I dreamed that I saw the faces of Persephone's captors. I think these faces may be the same people in hooded robes responsible for the taking of Lily. They certainly have the same description."

Hermes interrupted Aglaope. "Why would they be the same people? We know now that Haides was hidden, watching, directing Persephone's kidnappers when she was being taken."

Aglaope continued. 'Hermes, I saw the faces of the grae ladies that day. Persephone's captors were wearing cowled robes just the same as Qamar is describing the people at the dock and at the parties. For years I have closed my mind to this but at the villa on Samothrace I felt safe and relaxed. I am sure this is why I dreamed of what I have suppressed all of those years. I am sure it was the sisters of Medusa."

Hannah, who seemed to have been muted by fear in wanting the safe return of her daughter spoke meekly, "These grae ladies, Aglaope, who are they, why would they take Lily?"

Mel answered, "Hannah, please listen. Do you remember long ago when I told you of how my childhood friend, Medusa was banished to an island in an altered physical state so hideous that no person could look upon her. Two of her sisters decided they would transform themselves over with the same hideous look to stay with her. This was Stheno and Euryale. They had the power to do this. They were both true goddesses but Medusa was born half mortal like Lily. Their parents Ceto and Phorcys sent three of their other children to guard the island where Medusa and her two sisters were banished to stay forever. Ceto and Phorcys have many children and these other three sent to guard the island. The three are referred to by all as the grae ladies."

"These other children were also three other sisters of Medusa. They were born with an affliction that made them old from birth. They shared an eye and a tooth between the three. While growing up on Olympus, I glimpsed them from a distance once. It was frightening. They were always dressed in cowled robes to hide how hideous they appeared. Calli saw them one time at closer distance and told mother and father that they were too frightening to look upon. The grae ladies have guarded this island of Medusa situated on the farthest western end of the Mediterranean Sea just past Libya. Sometimes the island is called the island of the Gorgades. It is where the other two gorgons have stayed after Medusa's beheading by Perseus. He carried her head back across the water that night, dropping blood which still can be found in the coral reefs. This red coral is a beautiful garnet color but soft compared to reef material. It is sometimes referred to as blood red coral by divers. This is the coral Chrys searches the sea bottom to harvest. What Aglaope is saying may well be correct since we were warned that Medusa's family want the souls returned that were given to Persephone from Medusa's island. This was reason behind the message from the note left on the gate to the underworld. It was left for us to read, warning us that they will take our half mortal family members for a kind of retribution. They may have taken Lily." Mel finished this account.

Hannah was still trying to digest the information overload she had listened to from everyone in the room. She was hearing very convincing reasons to believe what Mel had related to the group in the room so did not immediately comment on Mel's accounting of the past right away. The room was silent as each of them tried to come up with a solution.

Hannah spoke first. "I am going to hire someone to take me to that island to search it for my daughter. I will pay someone to help me get Lily back."

Hermes put both of his hands on Hannah's shoulders. "Hannah, he spoke, "No mortal can handle these grae ladies. Another point to consider is that we don't know for sure that it was them who actually took Lily nor had Lily taken. Mel, Calli and I will handle this. We will leave tonight for the island to see if there is any activity going on. I know that the two sisters that were actually gorgon-like rarely stray into areas of the island close to the shoreline. By calling the sisters gorgon-like I am referring to their snake features. That is the reason you cannot handle the gorgon sisters."

Hannah pulled away, "No Hermes, Lily is my daughter. If you think you are going to leave me here, I will find my own way to the island. I must be part of the rescue. I will go to her."

Mel spoke to Hermes to convince him to hear the reasons behind Hannah's plea. "Hermes, we took Hannah to the underworld to rescue her husbands soul. Do you remember how well she did when she tried to stay focused? She is strong. We taught her how to concentrate for the fast travel. What do you think? Lily is her daughter too."

Although Hannah waited for his answer she had already made her decision. He finally said, "I am not agreeing with it but won't prevent you from bringing her with us, Mel. You and Calli will have to be responsible for her. If something should happen…."

Hannah interrupted, "Nothing will happen, Hermes. I will do what you ask of me. What I won't do is stay here, not knowing if Lily is safe or not."

"I will see Ceto on Olympus tonight and we will leave by noon possibly for the island of the Gorgons tomorrow when I return," Hermes continued, "meanwhile Saon, I want you to see Chrys right away, tonight. Let him know what has transpired. I think if you and Chrys take his outboard boat and leave for the island tonight, we could all meet you there. Hannah and Lily will travel back here to the Villa using that mode of transportation rather than ours. We are assuming that Lily has been taken to that island, of course. I want you to find out any information about these three half mortals that may have been passed from Chrys to Zharah then from Zharah on to the grae ladies."

the VILLA

Again Hannah interrupted Hermes. "Why will you go to Olympus, Hermes, we don't have time for that."

"Hannah," said Hermes, "Ceto and Phorcys must be told what is happening. This problem with our family goes back centuries. They may not even be aware of what is happening. The island we will go to is off limits to anyone who values their life. At one time to step on to the island meant you would be turned to stone. People thought of it as a myth but it was very true. Since Medusa's death this has not happened to any person. Still her gorgon-like siblings would cause great harm to those who stumble upon their home. Along with their snake-like features they possess strong venom that solidifies the blood in a person's veins, hence you turn to stone. The two of Ceto's daughters live under the protection and watchful eye of three of Ceto's other daughters known as the grae ladies. These grae ladies are who we believe left the note on the gate to the underworld. They are doing this at the request of the two Gorgon sisters who cannot leave the island. The two sisters, Euryale and Stheno want the souls returned that we stole from them to give Persephone in trade for Jack's soul. Now do you understand a little more of what we are up against?"

There was no answer Hannah could give to Hermes at this time. For the first time in over sixteen years Hannah felt like she was coming undone again. She knew she must keep strong for Lily. She pushed aside the rising horror she felt was her daughter's fate. If Lily were being held captive on this island she would definitely see the two gorgon sisters. Lily could not know that she should not look upon them. The punishment for this would be certain death. A whole day had passed since Lily was missing. This was the second night her daughter was in harms way. Hannah knew she would not rest and for sure she would not sleep this night. She spent the night hoping for Hermes to return from Olympus earlier than was planned. Nightmares from the underworld invaded Hannah's rest. She dreamed of the ferryman from the River Styx, chasing her and Lily. Hands grabbed her feet as she stepped on them while trying to reach the gate to leave the underworld. Just as her and Lily finally started to breathe the cool air from outside, hands began grabbing at her again. Hannah screamed herself out of the night terror waking to see Arabella gently shaking her to help her wake up. Hannah had fallen asleep until eleven the next morning. She slept through the night when she should have left with Saon and Chrys for the island.

22

Close to midday Hermes returned as promised with an update that indeed information was carelessly being passed from Zharah to all who showed interest in the three half mortals who had newly taken up residence at the Zeus villa. It was not intended as a vindictive act toward them but more as gossip among the younger immortals on Olympus. With that discussed and then fact that Hannah failed to leave with Saon in the night, Hermes suggested that Hannah would definitely ride with Chrys and Saon on the outboard motor boat on the return trip to the villa. Hannah had argued that no one awakened her to leave with Saon. She felt she won the right to fast travel with Melpomene to the island of the Gorgons. She may have won Hermes over to her side with the decision for now and would argue later for fast travel back to Jeddah despite the arrangement of the waiting boat at the island. The trip to the island seemed to go well. Hannah focused on being part of Mel again as she did long ago when they travelled to the island of flowers to retrieve Jack's soul. At this time Hannah felt as if her heart was in her throat. Lily had to be okay. She had to be here on this strange island of the Gorgons.

Everything on the island looked like stone; even the color of the trees looked starved from a lack of water. They had a dry chalky quality as if everything in sight were coated in a layer of clay dust. The trees all looked dead and most were without leaves. Whatever direction Hannah looked showed an apparent absence of life. Along the shoreline Hannah noticed how dry and bare the land appeared. While first seeing the island before stepping on the shore she thought it may be erosion from the wind and water. As they walked inland there was a lot of exposed rock. Hannah did not see any grass or vegetation. An absence of birds singing was very noticeable to Hannah as she surveyed the pale clay colour of everything in sight. The only word to describe Hannah's impression of the landscape was lifeless. The island was covered in hills and canyons, with paths leading off in every direction. Anyone could be hiding almost anywhere, even just a few feet from where they stood. Clearly, in this first part of the trek there wasn't a sign of life or of Lily.

Mel told Hannah earlier that Chrys would meet them on the island. Hannah had not met Chrys yet. This person was the reason Lily was not safe at the Villa with her at this moment. Lily had been going out every evening to meet Chrys and his friends. Hannah had really believed that Lily was retiring to her bedroom because of the heat and the time difference with her usual sleep time in Forgotten Cove. Lily had gone to her bed for the night at the same early hour she had been retiring since arriving in Jeddah. There was a lot to think about but Hannah was only concerned for her daughter's safety at this moment. Calli and Hermes walked ahead of her making up part of the group from the villa.

After a five minute walk along the shoreline, Chrys and Saon met them at the only boat landing. They had arrived several hours ago sometime during the night on Chrys's rigid inflatable boat with eight two-hundred and fifty horsepower motors. Hannah heard Saon bragging to the others about the speed of the watercraft. This was considered one of the necessities in life that Chrys should own for his travel up and down the coast of the Red Sea in search of the red coral he dove for. Chrys had decided it was a good idea to use this mode of transportation for Lily rather than the immortals quick flight. He would transport Lily and her mother back to Jeddah.

Maybe if this were under different circumstances, Hannah would be more receptive to Chrys. He was polite, soft spoken and it was obvious he was very worried. Hannah politely nodded at the introduction, saying to the group, "Can we get moving?"

Hermes organized the group to push forward with Mel, Hannah and Saon following behind them as Calli and Chrys flanked him. The entourage proceeded across the unpleasant hilly landscape. Calli collaborated with Chrys yesterday before the departure from the villa. He had learned from Ceto years ago that the home of the Gorgon sisters was less than a mile from the boat landing. Hermes instructed Mel to keep Hannah well behind them in case there was a problem with the grae ladies. He fully expected there was going to be some type of altercation. They had also decided before leaving the villa to meet back on Olympus instead of in Jeddah where Lily and Hannah would stay with Mnemosyne for a week. It would be a safe destination for the mother and daughter. It might be the right time to introduce Lily to family members on Olympus. This would also serve to separate Lily from Chrys a short time to focus on her layering skills.

Calli saw the grae ladies first and quickly alerted the group to remain quiet. They were walking slowly about fifty feet ahead of them dragging a huge sack across the rough terrain. Chrys volunteered that he would question them since they were part of his ancestral family. As Chrys was walking forward one of the grae ladies dumped the contents from the sack. Out of the sack tumbled an unconscious Lily. It was more than a mother could bear. Hannah moved quickly to get ahead. She quickly ran past them to attack her daughter's kidnappers. One of the grae ladies grabbed Hannah by her throat and easily lifted her off her a few feet from the ground. She rose up to her full height and threw Hannah at the rocky edge of the small hill. A sickening thud was heard as Hannah's head struck a sharpened rock. She tumbled over the edge and was gone from sight as if she had never been on the island. Chrys grabbed for the precious contents of the sack while Hermes and Calli become airborne to distract the ladies. Mel and Saon rushed downward, down the rocky ledges to find Hannah. They found her in a crumpled heap back down the path where they entered the island not an hour before. Their only thought was to get Hannah to the boat. The group had to get off of the island quickly. Chrys carried the unconscious Lily to the outboard. He arrived just as Saon and Mel were gently laying the bloodied Hannah on a tarp in the boat.

Chrys yelled back to Mel that they have to head quickly to the private clinic at the bottom of Olympus. Hannah should be taken to it immediately. Chrys had half dragged Lily down the same path toward their landing site. Chrys knew that he must get Lily off of the island before the Gorgon sisters see her. He loaded her into the boat along side of her unconscious mother cradled gently in Mel's arms. Chrys started the powerful engines, backed out and headed north-east to Olympus. He knew speed was very important at this time. Hermes and Calli looked down moments later as they paused in their quick flight. They would go on ahead to Olympus and meet the speeding boat at this clinic. Mel looked at Hannah whose face was covered with bloody clots and clay. Hannah's mouth was agape.

Her sightless eyes stared at Mel, eyes that could not see the tears fall from the eyes of the beautiful Muse of Tragedy.

Lily was beginning to come awake in Saon's arms as she struggled to become aware of her surroundings. She was panicking as she looked from Chrys to Mel then at her mother. Lily stared at the open water and again at Mel questioning what had happened to her.

"Lily, you are safe with us now. We are on our way to Olympus. Your mother has had an accident. She will be okay, Lily." Mel was trying to talk quickly to get Lily's attention before she tried to escape the boat. Chrys shouted back to them that they would be less than a few hours from land and the small clinic at the bottom of Olympus.

The following day and many hours later than the arrival at the clinic the small group gathered back at the Zeus family home on Olympus. Mel tried to stay inside of her mind. The agony Lily was experiencing was unbearable for Mel who felt as if she should be a shield for her against all of life's insults that inflicted themselves on such an innocent as Lily. Melpomene thought about the earlier conversation with her mother on Olympus. She begged her mother to join Lily in her vigil. Mnemosyne usually kept her distant demeanour steady until Mel ask of her to share the information she knew of future events regarding Lily's mother Hannah. Mnemosyne flew into a rage.

"Melpomene," she began, "you know that we must never interfere with the direction of what happens at the human level of life. I rarely, if ever would tell a half mortal or a mortal of a memory of an event that has not happened yet. I cannot disclose the outcome of the coma Hannah exists in right now."

"Mother, I love Lily and Hannah as much as the family that was taken from me by Demeter. I care about them as part of our family. It was my daughter who interfered in Hannah's life. She did not ask to lose her husband all of those years ago."

"Melpomene, if the incident at Forgotten Cove had not happened and you had not met Hannah, then Lily would have never been in your life. Am I right about this? You brought Hannah to the island of flowers. It was you who introduced her to Hermes. Do I need to continue?" Mnemosyne held Mel in her intimidating gaze.

"No mother, you are right." Mel felt as a small child being chastised by her mother right now.

"Anyway, Mel, I wanted you here to tell you that I have already spoken to Lily this early morning at the clinic. I don't often leave our home but I felt this was important. I told Lily that she would be seeing her mother again." Mnemosyne shared this bit of information with her worried daughter.

Melpomene grasped her mother's delicate hands and pressed her lips gently to them. "Mother, thank you for telling Lily just what will happen in the future to put her mind at ease about her mother."

Mnemosyne continued. "Mel, I said Lily would see her mother again. I did not tell her when or where this was to happen. It exists only in the memory of what has not yet happened to Lily and Hannah. It is not for all of us to know if it will be in this realm of existence or the heavenly realm. It has been written but not yet lived."

Mnemosyne turned back to the flowers she was attending to when Mel arrived mid morning. Mel knew not to push this conversation further. She must be happy at least with knowing the small relief Mnemosyne provided Lily with. Mel knew she must return immediately to the private clinic where Hannah was handed over to the care of the very best medical staff on this earth. Mel had called in neurosurgeons from France to perform the necessary surgery to relieve the increasing swelling from the haematoma suffered by Hannah arising from striking her head on the rocks. Hannah had been taken immediately from the island of the Gorgons to the clinic down the mountain from Olympus by Mel on Chrys's fast moving speed boat. If Hannah were not attended to promptly as she had been then she surely would have died. The clinic would stabilize Hannah further in preparation for the journey to Forgotten Cove. Ellie had been informed of the accident. Preparations were being arranged by Ellie and Mel at Hannah's house for her care at home. This care would be overseen by Ellie along with several shifts of nurses attending Hannah twenty-four hours a day. The preparations were being made for staff and equipment to aid in her recovery so Hannah would be comfortable in her own home when she awoke from her coma.

Later as Melpomene released Lily from her hug, she looked at Lily and saw great pain in her eyes. Mel could read the pain of disbelief, a pain she often saw in her own eyes as she stared into mirrors.

"Mel, I tried to layer into my mother earlier and she is not responding. Is she brain damaged? What am I doing wrong?" Lily sobbed through tears.

"No Lily you are not doing anything wrong. You are close to your mother and want her to know that you are here with her. When a person is in a coma, it is not the same as being asleep and unaware of another presence. We layer into people who have a space open, like the window sill for us to wait then to enter. Do you remember our talk about it? A person in a coma does not have this window sill, this unused space. Their mind is busy, almost cluttered, with getting to know their new surroundings. They are trying to find out if any other people exist in this new space. Between the light layer of afterlife and the dark layer of this life on earth exists another layer. You were told how life can be compared to the layers in folded fabric. The grey layer is between life and death right here while we are on earth. It is a layer, even as immortals and half mortals, we can never enter. We can not interfere with or have any type of intervention on behalf of the mortal's journey through this layer. The person walking in this layer is fragile. They must face the dark layer and the light layer alone. They must decide to go on into the light layer of the afterlife or return to the dark layer here on earth to continue their journey. Your mother is safe. In the grey layer you do not feel pain. There is only thought. There may be unfinished business for her to consider. You will be the unfinished business. Your mother has to decide to stay with you for a longer time on earth. We can't make that decision for her."

Lily considered this for a moment and then spoke. "Mel, will my mother blame me and be angry and not want to return? It is entirely my fault for going out that night to the yacht to be with Chrys."

"Lily, you should not place fault or blame right now. It was my decision to let her come with us to find you after you were kidnapped. I knew Hannah was mortal. I knew she was agitated and not able to focus even while we were on the fast travel. She was so worried about you. I also knew if I didn't let her accompany us then she may try to find you alone and may end up being taken too. So let's not lay blame. Let's concentrate on getting her stable and moved home to Forgotten Cove."

Lily gave her a weakened smile and an even weaker hug. "Yes, we must focus on my mother and save the fault finding for another day."

24

The next three weeks were critical in getting the swelling under control that put Hannah into her present state. Mel worked around the clock with Ellie in hiring the best care for Hannah's house. The bedroom Hannah had shared with Jack now looked like the finest intensive care unit of the best hospital on earth. Mel did not spare any expense on equipment and nurses.

A full month later back home in Forgotten Cove, Lily could smell the fresh rot of the decaying leaves hanging in the air. It was a beautiful early fall day. She loved the crispness of the autumn air in Forgotten Cove. The leaves were every shade of brown, red and yellow. They danced the dance of death slowly toward the ground layering it with their protective blanket. This coloured blanket made up of nature's leaves would cover Forgotten Cove in preparation for the winter snowfalls that would begin shortly. Lily stood back from the cool sandy beach in an effort to see the lone figure standing on the bluff. She had stood here on this spot many times growing up in Forgotten Cove. She tried to make out if it was a man or a woman but the figure could not be made out as to which gender. Lily sensed, rather than saw who this person was. Her heightened awareness had improved enough that she now knew when someone was watching her as if she could hear them looking at her. Her senses were becoming sharper with every passing day. Lily knew this was not an invasion of her privacy with someone watching her but it was a measure taken for her safety.

This last year had been life changing for Lily. She had become very close with Ikram and Qamar. They were the sisters she never had while growing up in Forgotten Cove. She now felt closer to her father and Mel. Lily felt that her father, Hermes did care for her as any cherished daughter would be cared for. Chrys had come into her life. Lily decided at her young age that he was to be her life's mate. She hoped that he may feel the same as her too, that it would be a forever relationship. Hopefully mother could understand all of this.

Lily felt the gentle touch of a hand as it came to rest on her shoulder. She turned to see Mel. Lily knew Mel had come to tell her it was time to be going. She could see that Mel wanted to have a talk with her.

"Lily, I realise that today is a sad day for you. You need to be strong for what the future may bring you. I was around your age when I lost my friend Medusa on Olympus. It shaped me into who I am today. This will shape you into the woman you will become. Your mother will at least have an opportunity to return. Her mind is now in a restful place. Be happy for her." They walked as they carried on this conversation slowly into the village center.

The small stone chapel stood in a grove of oak trees that were planted over a century ago when the chapel was built. The stone structure had seen many people pass through its doors from this world. Today it would see a gathering of prayers for Hannah to recover from any memory loss and return to a conscious state from her catatonic like existence.

the VILLA

Her dead husband, Jack Gallegar would live forever in the memories of the people in Forgotten Cove. His family were part of the fabric that made this village complete. This caring was now extended to Hannah and her daughter. People who loved Jack, as his friend Ellie did, took comfort in believing that Jack was looking out for Hannah from somewhere. Ellie could see that Hannah was definitely not present in the body of the woman she and several home nurses cared for around the clock. The people of Forgotten Cove had come to accept Hannah through the years even though they felt she was not quite the same as they were in hardiness to live the life of a fisherman.

Inside of the chapel there were a few school friends Lily had grown up with in Forgotten Cove. Ellie and her family were seated in the family section of the chapel. It felt so much like a funeral. Lily held tightly to Mel's hand. It was Mel who had become like a mother figure in her life. The service was short. Lily had a lot on her mind right now. She would miss her mother. Lily had been told all of her life by her mother to always remember that life was for the living. Lily knew she would take this advice tomorrow but today she wanted say good-bye to her mother just for awhile. Lily also remembered the promise she made her mother that she would never be separated from her. She felt sad about wanting to leave Forgotten Cove but knew it wouldn't be forever. Mnemosyne had assured her of a meeting with her mother again some day in her future.

Lily decided that this meant her mother would walk again and regain her life as her mother. This eased a bit of the pain Lily felt for causing her mother's coma. The people of Forgotten Cove had contributed generously to a fund to support the care of her mother. They gave generously to help pay for the equipment needed to keep her mother at home where she was tended to around the clock. Lily was grateful that the people of Forgotten Cove along with Mel had relieved her of any worry of enough of an income to care for her mother.

Mnemosyne had taken Lily aside for their talk as Mel had done. This was to help Lily to understand her mother's state. She explained to Lily how a coma is another layer of existence in our life. We can still see the conscious world but something very comforting is drawing us forward into the many layers of black shadows that fade into grey shadows, then to a final clear white light. Mnemosyne told Lily that her mother was already in the grey shadow layer so was still in a safe position to return. Mnemosyne also tried to make Lily understand that Jack had only reached the pale grey shadowy outer layer before the white light. This was because he had such a traumatic end. He wanted to stay in this world. Jack kept wandering between the black layers to the grey layers then back again toward the black even though he should have entered the white layer long before Lily's birth. Jack was not ready to leave this world when Aglaope decided he would. Lily learned from Mnemosyne that she gave Jack and Hannah her gift of a memory in these layers so they could communicate across the shadow layers until Jack could finally say good-bye to Hannah. Hannah would return from her coma after Jack moved on. It was known only to Mnemosyne that Jack was drawing Hannah closer to the lighter grey layer and so closer toward the white light. Mnemosyne realized that Hannah was not aware of the layered spaces she had entered. She did not understand that dark layers in this place were for those who want to return to consciousness. Hannah would learn this as all others who have spent time in this layer had learned before her.

Mnemosyne decided not to tell Lily that she had actually spoken to Hannah in this grey layer. It was better for now that Lily think Mnemosyne was speaking to her about her mother from her vast great experiences in others lives. Lily must never know that Mnemosyne had actually spoken with her mother in her present state.

25

Earlier when Hannah had listened to what Mnemosyne was telling her about the situation she was in right now she couldn't understand completely. Her mind felt very confused. Blackness surrounded her in every direction. The black was complete and sometimes appeared to be glistening with something wet. It felt solid, yet yielded softly to her touch. It was flat and again she sensed the roundness of what she thought were like walls around her. Hannah reached out and touched the blackness again. It felt cool and wet. She was surprised when her hand came away dry. Where was she? She felt as if she had entered a void, an area of empty space but it somehow felt so crowded. The space was not crowded with people but was crowded with layer upon layer of blackness, the absence of light. Hannah felt she needed to keep moving until sense could be made of all of it. She started to sense she was not alone in this place. Hannah tried to remember if someone had just told her this.

Hannah called out to the spaces that were beginning to appear, "Is anyone here? I think I am lost. Please help me."

She waited. No answer came. Hannah was becoming acutely aware of the absence of sound and smell. She felt close to a state of panic when she realized this place felt like nothingness. Hannah tried to reason for a moment that "nothingness" was not really a word or a place but was the only word that came to mind for where Hannah felt she was right now.

Ahead of her appeared a grey area slowly coming into focus as she moved forward. That area caught her attention. It seemed as if it were pulsing in and out of her focus. It appeared that layers of grey fabric were moving slowly in the gentlest breeze. As she moved toward the fluid folds Hannah began sensing that someone she had loved was waiting there for her. They were waiting for her to come toward them, into their grey layers.

"Who are you?" Hannah spoke aloud. She heard her own voice speaking in a low whisper. It sounded alien to her. It was very calm as if there wasn't a reason to be in a hurry or to panic at not knowing where she was right now. She sensed that it was peaceful as well as safe here.

A disembodied voice told her that the person next to her was Jack. It sounded like Jack had just spoken to her. Hannah began to feel now as if she were in a safe place. Jack had always kept her safe at home. She wanted to think about home and Lily but that required more effort than Hannah could spend at this time. She moved toward the grey coloured layers cautiously. Maybe her life with Lily was all a beautiful dream. Maybe Jack was still here with her wherever they were at this time. Hannah felt a little confused but did not have the energy to question why she was feeling confused at hearing Jack speak.

"Jack. Jack, is this really you?" Hannah felt as if her voice was a whisper off in the distance with each word she spoke rather than coming from inside of her.

"Hannah, I have been waiting such a long time for you. I need to talk with you. I do understand now that it wasn't you on the boat the night of the storm. What happened to me that night? I feel so lost here in this place. I am staying here in this grey layer to wait for you. I did see you give me my soul back to the sea to help me find my resting place, but Hannah; I am waiting for you to join me. We can go toward the lighter layers together."

Hannah slowly moved closer to the shades of grey, close enough to see the ghostly figure of the man she had loved as much as life itself. She had married him all those years ago in Forgotten Cove because of his beautiful smile. When she reached out her hand to touch him, Hannah felt a warm tingling on her fingertips, not really a touch of his skin. She began to realize where she walked today was a world meant for experiencing only the senses. It was not part of the earth. Hannah was trying to remember why Jack was not with her on earth. Jack left her. He died long ago on the fishing boat when it crashed into the rocks. *Does this mean that I am dead now too?* Hannah wondered about this.

There was Hermes after Jack. Yes there was a life after Jack died. Hermes gave her Lily. He came into her life so unexpectedly. Yes, Hermes gave her Lily. Hannah kept repeating to herself that Hermes gave her Lily. It hurt her head to think of it. She knew she had Lily to care for but it was confusing to her that Lily was not here with her. Hannah wanted to return to Lily. She was not finished yet on earth. Lily needed her to be a mother to her for many more years.

"Jack, you must go on. I need to return to my daughter Lily. I will join you later," pleaded Hannah. Hannah became aware of a heaviness beginning to fill her head. It felt similar to the pain she called a dull ache. It didn't hurt a lot, it was just there.

Jack kept on talking to her, "Please Hannah, stay with me a small while then I will go further into the light to wait for you."

Hannah looked at the man she had loved so completely and answered him forgetting Lily again, "Yes Jack, I will stay with you awhile."

Hannah reached out to hold the hand of her dear Jack only to sense the feel of a silkiness brushing against her hand. She followed him toward the brighter grey layers. Hannah could see his face more clearly now and wanted to caress the jaw line she loved to touch so many years ago. If she walked farther into the paler grey layers, Hannah was sure she would see Jack wholly. She moved slowly toward the pale grey.

Lily stared at her mother from her tear-stained face. She looked at the lifeless body hooked up to the medical equipment. The machines could not be the only reason her mother was breathing. It was so shallow. Was this because her mother was really dead except for the machines breathing for her?

Lily's body shook with sobs. "I didn't mean for this to happen to you, mother." She reached out to hold her mothers hand but Lily was afraid to touch her mother in case it would interrupt the machines that gave her mother the life support needed at this time. Lily turned to leave. She needed to go to the bluffs for a walk to clear her mind. As she closed the door behind her she did not hear Hannah whisper quietly the word, Jack.

LILY HAD MADE SOME HARD decisions in the last two months. She was not sure right now why or if she even wanted to keep this house in Forgotten Cove. Hermes and Mel both advised her that she must keep close ties with Ellie and so she must keep the house to enable her mother to recover in her own home. Mel assured Lily that she would always have a home at the villa in Jeddah and on Olympus with her new extended family. This was a comfort. Lily would somehow divide her time with this place and Jeddah so she could be with Chrys. The walk today up to the bluffs did clear her head. Lily knew she must be strong for her mother and stay in a positive frame of mind. It seemed as if her mother's coma would never come to an end.

Later the same afternoon the sun was hanging heavy in the western sky. A tearful Ellie was hugging Lily tightly. "Lily, you will always be like a daughter for me. I will always be here and take care of your mother and her house for you. It will be ready for you whenever you want to return to Forgotten Cove". This was Ellie's reaction to Lily's decision to leave Forgotten Cove shortly after the New Year to help Ikram with her wedding as planned shortly before Ikram and Saon left for Samothrace.

There was such a lot to think about. Lily had made a plan earlier in the day that she would stay with Ikram and Saon on the island of Samothrace for a few weeks before making any permanent decisions about her future. They were preparing for a late spring wedding that she was asked to be a part of. She looked out the window, up to the bluffs. She could make out the lone figure in long robes still standing there, waiting for her. Lily hugged Ellie back. She told Ellie she would see her a while later that she needed another solitary walk on the bluffs.

26

Forgotten Cove became silent with falling snow muffling out sound. Lily cared for her mother along with the nurses. She watched everyday to see any sign of winter giving up its iron grip on the landscape. The icicles that hung from the eaves of Hannah's house slowly began to get shorter from the continuous dripping of water into the snow piled under the window facing the bluffs. Snow piled on the side of the roads began recede. A few brave birds sat outside of the windows noisily telling Lily that they would stay if she put seeds out for them. The path to Ellie's house was well worn. Mel had come a week ago to stay for a month. A few weeks later Lily needed to be outside. Lily looked upward as she walked toward the bluffs. As she came closer she could see the lone figure gesture with an outstretched hand to receive her. Chrys smiled at her. He gathered her close to him as she buried herself safely in his familiar arms. They stood together without speaking for awhile.

"Chrys, I need to know if you or anyone you have spoken with feels that I am the reason for what has happened to my mother." Lily looked deep into Chrys's eyes to search out an answer. "I need to know everything that happened on that island. Nobody has spoken to me about it. They are treating me as if I am so fragile."

"Lily, you should talk further with Mel. She is the closest to you aside from your mother's friend, Ellie. I want you to take all the time you need to be here in Forgotten Cove. Soon you will go to visit Samothrace for the wedding. When you come back here again to Forgotten Cove please stay with your mother awhile. I will wait for you on the yacht however long it takes. We are the new beginning for both of our families. It has been centuries since that terrible event happened on Olympus that ended Medusa's life as a mortal. It was too soon for her to leave earth. Somehow I feel that you and I will one day have a daughter to give back to the earth in her honor." Chrys stopped speaking a moment so Lily would have time to digest his proposal.

"Chrys, are you asking me to marry you?" Lily countered meekly.

"Please Lily," Chrys said, "wait until the time is right to answer. I want you to be sure. I must go now. I will visit you on Samothrace when you arrive there. I will see you before the month long preparations are over. Saon asked me to stand for the wedding too, as his best man. Now I must leave. I have received word of a large deposit of red coral north of Jeddah that I want to investigate."

Lily stared into the eyes of the man she loved and could see that her answer would be yes to a life with Chrys. For the first time in a long while Lily felt the world was moving forward and was going to be good for her again.

As she run down the bluffs, Lily felt the cold wind trying to keep pace with her. She felt as if the world was turning again for her just as the earth was transforming itself into spring. Lily wanted to share her news with Mel and with Ellie first. The two stood outside on Ellie's deck deep in conversation when she almost ran them over.

"Whoa!" Ellie grabbed her in one of her motherly hugs. "What has got you so light footed? Wait a minute young lady. I think I can guess. It is exactly the same look I saw on your mother's face all those years ago when she come to tell me that Jack Gallegar asked her to marry him. How close am I to the truth Lily?" Ellie gave Mel a conspiratorial wink.

"Oh Ellie, I can't get anything past you. Yes, Chrys has asked me to marry him," Lily hopped from foot to foot as she answered Ellie.

Mel and Ellie reached out together to hug Lily again. Mel told her they must keep themselves in this positive state for the duration of her mother's convalescence. The day ended on a happy note for the three. It was the first natural smile that came this easily from the three for the past few months.

Inside of Hannah's house the nurse attending Hannah heard a faint whisper. It sounded like someone calling out the name of Jack. The nurse would report this to Mel and Lily as she filled them in on Hannah's progress with her shift report later.

Lily had already asked Mel earlier in the week to tell her what happened on the island. She expressed her fear the grae ladies would try again to take her to the two remaining Gorgon sisters. Lily wanted to ask about the island months ago but she was afraid of what she would be told.

Melpomene took Lily by her hand and sat her in Hannah's favourite reading chair. She began, "You should be very comfortable. Lily, we will talk this out until everything is understood completely by you." Lily nodded in consent to begin.

"Lily, Hermes and I had you and the others followed a few times to the yacht. We knew the four of you were visiting Chrys. You are young and so it was natural to seek out people your own age to have fun. We tried to keep watch to be sure you were safe. Hermes did speak to Saon about his taking you to the yacht and off to Morocco."

Mel raised her hand to silence Lily as she tried to speak in her own defence. "Let me finish, Lily. It was inevitable that you would take advantage of the fast flights for travel. That is what it is intended to be used for. No one is angry. It is certainly not the fault of any of the four of you that you want to enjoy your half mortal status. However none of us knew that the grae ladies were watching in Jeddah and in Tangier. Actually we found information through our sources that they were stalking Ikram, Qamar and you, Lily. Qamar mentioned several times to Saon that she felt uncomfortable with the hooded people at the villa in Tangier. Because of their size she thought they were men wearing hooded robes when they were actually the three grae ladies, sisters of the two remaining Gorgons and also sisters of Medusa. The ladies were tailing you everywhere you went in Jeddah, waiting for an opportunity to grab any one of you. When you went out the night you were abducted, the sisters were waiting for such an event to happen. They made you unconscious using chloroform, put you in a large duffle bag in a trunk and stowed it safely in the bottom of their boat. From what we can tell they were not travelling that quickly. They must have arrived on the island shortly before we did. Your mother pushed us to find you immediately. We contacted Chrys to take your mother with Saon on his outboard motor boat. We thought it was the best way to get your mother to the island. As it turned out she opted for us taking her on our fast flight. We met Chrys and Saon at the dock of the island. Hermes and Calli accompanied us. There is only one dusty path on that island so we followed it to the top of a rocky precipice. Your mother saw the duffle bag the grae ladies had stuffed you inside of. Next you were being dumped out of it. Even I was unsure that you were still alive. It was more than your mother could bear. Without warning your mother run past all of us to help you. One of the grae ladies grabbed her by her throat and threw her over the ledge of the hill like an old rag. Chrys grabbed you away from them as Hermes and Calli fought off the two ladies to distract them from Chrys rescuing you. Saon and I run to the bottom of the hill to help your mother. We found her in a heap at the bottom with quite a bloody gash in her head. That was when Chrys decided we would take your mother in his boat and head for the small clinic at the bottom of Olympus with you and Saon in tow."

"My sister Calli is very gifted at persuasion so used this attribute to have the grae ladies meet her on Olympus at Phorcys family home later that week. Hermes and Calli then fast travelled to the clinic to meet the rest of us."

Mel paused. Lily was assessing the information before she spoke. "Mel if someone was watching then why didn't they stop me when I went to the yacht that night? I am not saying I was right to go but it would have been a different outcome."

"Lily you will have to take that responsibility on your own shoulders. Our priority is your mother's recovery right now. You have been told you will see her again by Mnemosyne so with this information you can rest a little easier." Mel thought before speaking again, "I think we have to move on as if your mother were in a conscious state. You go ahead to both Samothrace and Anthemoessa to help with the wedding preparations. Let Ikram and Aglaope know of your wonderful news with the betrothal to Chrys."

Mel paused again, looked at Lily and smiled. "Lily, this event, this betrothal between a descendant of the Ceto and Phorcys house to a descendant of the Mnemosyne and Zeus house is of great importance to the world of immortals, half mortals like you and to the mortals on earth. It is a new beginning to heal a lot of bitter memories amongst the immortals. Some of these memories have influenced the wars and genocides in history. This is a chance to heal man's inhumanity to man."

Lily spoke so quietly with her answer that Mel had to lean toward her to hear what she was saying. "Mel, I don't know what to say. I am a small town girl in my heart. What I mean to say is that I grew up here in Forgotten Cove. It was a lot for me to understand that I was half mortal, that I can have my life ended but not by aging. It is a lot you are asking me to understand when you say that Chrys and I will have such an impact on humanity. I feel a little frightened."

'Lily, there is nothing to fear. Your father, Hermes will see that you are well educated in the art of layering and in the fast travel. We also need to discuss your layering. Lily, you are falling short of obligations to mortals in need of help. I can only think of one person you have actually helped by layering. This was when you were a younger girl. Do you remember the boy in the wheelchair on the beach all those years ago?"

Mel continued after a nod from Lily. "You have never returned to him. You did not take the time to find him and visit again. Remember he is trapped inside of his mind. You must layer him again to give him new memories of your life. The gift of layering is just what it is, a gift. You must share this gift with those who need it."

"Oh, Mel I never thought of it this way. I have been so selfish thinking of all the parties and clothes rather than thinking of others. I will begin to find those people I can help."

Mel continued, "Don't be hard on yourself. There is nothing wrong in wanting to enjoy your youth. As far as your marriage to Chrys, this will all be discussed between Mnemosyne and Ceto. They will take charge of everything on Olympus. Your mother will be with us by that time and Ellie will be included too. None of us will take you from your comfort zone Lily, not ever."

"I understand Mel. I was thinking to leave soon, maybe as soon as tomorrow to stay with Ikram. I want to help with her wedding plans. Is this going to be okay with Ellie and your plans?"

"I think both Ellie and I would agree that you should go to help Ikram. The last thing we will discuss, Lily, is the wedding of Ikram and Saon. As you have already learned from Hermes, in the immortal world we don't usually have a marriage ceremony. This leaves our lives open to be of assistance whenever we are called upon for different events and to use our talents for our lives to have a positive impact on others. However, I did marry Achelous in a ceremony. It turned out to be a disaster. I can hardly be in the same room as he is in. My mother and father never married and we have a stable, happy family. Hermes did not marry your mother or Saon's mother or Arabella and there does not seem to be a problem with any of the involved people. Ikram and Saon are telling the world by marrying in a ceremony that they have no intention of ever seeking another partner. It is more common with the younger immortals and half mortals to marry that way. They fit into social situations easier than if they were not a couple. This marriage of my granddaughter Ikram will be significant to the family in healing Aglaope's relationship with me. Her two sisters keep distant from her and from me as well because of the aggression she has displayed toward me in the past. When you get to know Ikram's mom a little better, I am sure you will see a person going through major changes for the sake of her daughter. Lily, now tell me, where will they meet with you? They are aware that you have never been to Anthemoessa."

Lily responded to Mel, telling her of plans to meet the two of them in Athens where they would scour the shops for tulle, netting, silks and whatever else is needed for the wedding. Mel could see how eager Lily was to distract herself from the stress of the last few months with settling her mother into a routine with the caregivers.

It was a heavy burden for any young girl. Lily's world had turned upside down in this past year. She transformed from a young woman living in a small seaside village to having the modern world and all of the fantasy worlds open their doors to her.

27

The trip to Athens was slow. Lily wanted it this way so she could use the time soul searching. Lily chose to fly using Aegean Air from Montreal. At this time Lily wanted to surround herself with people. She chose to use a tour bus service to Montreal to connect with her flight to Athens. While in transit Lily thought over just where her life was heading. Sure, the parties every night were fun but Melpomene had struck a raw nerve with her when she mentioned to Lily that her half mortal life was a gift to be used for the benefit of others less fortunate in life. Many hours after boarding the airliner the plane descended into Athens a full day and a half after leaving Forgotten Cove. During the flight Lily had made the challenge for learning her crafts the biggest priority in her life. A taxi whisked her away to Ermou Street. Lily laughed when the taxi driver told her the English translation for Ermou Street was Hermes Street. Aglaope and Ikram arrived ahead of her and booked her a suite at the Electra Hotel. They assured her that it was a very luxurious hotel. It was a great area for them to shop for wedding fabric and gifts for the guests of the family. This was exactly what

Lily needed at this time. The three spent the next week seeing the sights and enjoying the food. The threesome did not bring up recent events with Lily being taken by the grae ladies, however they did discuss Hannah's coma. Aglaope assured Lily that her mother was in good hands.

For the next five days the trio shopped and ate in every restaurant in the area. They behaved as any tourist in Athens enjoying all the sights to see. Lily relaxed, finally accepting that these people were now family. They cared for her. When the three left Athens for Anthemoessa, Lily was made to feel quite comfortable at the island home of Ikram and her mother. The two were very gracious in sharing their home with Lily on their island of flowers. For the first few days it was relaxing and just enjoyment of the splendid gardens. Flowers landscaped the entire area. In every direction Lily could see, fields of flowers carpeted the earth. The smell of this island was so fragrant. Aglaope showed great concern for Lily having to deal with her mother's coma and the wedding at the same time in her life. Aglaope accommodated this by her sympathetic listening to Lily telling her of her mothers care. Lily told Aglaope and Ikram stories of how it was for her growing up in Forgotten Cove with a single parent.

Tomorrow would begin the preparations at Saon's family home for the wedding less than three weeks from today. It was so exciting. Lily had learned a few great ideas for planning her own wedding in the future from Ikram and Aglaope. She was bursting inside with wanting to tell everyone she talked with about Chrys's proposal to her but made the decision to announce it with him by her side shortly after Ikram and Saon were married.

The trip was short to Samothrace. It was a lot like Athens and a lot like Anthemoessa with all of its natural beauty. In every direction a person looked there was an abundance of wildflowers. The sun shone gently and the birds sang happy songs. It was a peaceful island. When Lily, Ikram and Aglaope arrived they were treated as royalty by everyone they met. She knew this was genuine just by seeing the adoring looks people from the small village gave them. The three weeks preparation were so busy with wardrobes, food and decoration that it ended before the girls rested. Hermes was busy with Rhene preparing for the actual events of the ceremony. Rhene was also very busy with Aglaope in overseeing the preparations for seating the guests of honour. Preparing food for the biggest celebration the island would have for many years to come was an enormous task for Rhene. Hundreds of people wove garlands using the wild grasses on the island. The flowers used and woven into these garlands were picked by every child available on the island. Baskets brimming with early summer fruits filled the more than one hundred tables. The tables each had a handmade lantern placed on the pale mint green netting used as table covers. The choices of the mint green netting come from Ikram and Saon. They chose small purple violets made into tiny garlands to surround the base of each of the lanterns on every table. Every other decision for décor was shared between Aglaope and Rhene. Several giant spits roasted a variety of meats that dripped juices down to huge metal pots of vegetables set into slow burning coals. It would truly be a feast.

All of this on the wedding day gave time to Lily to greet Chrys before helping Ikram dress for her big day. Chrys was excited to share with Lily that an entourage from Tangier had arrived. She would be excited to see Zharah later again but told Chrys he must wait for the ceremony to end before she would join him to meet the group from Tangier. Lily told Chrys they would make their announcement on their engagement at this same time after the ceremony had ended. Excitedly Lily dressed for the wedding carefully then joined Qamar to help Ikram who was so excited by now she barely was in control of herself.

"Lily, Qamar, I want to thank you so much for everything you have done to help me. I am so happy that I may forget to thank the both of you later," chattered Ikram quickly.

Qamar answered for both of them. "We are so happy for you and Saon. Ikram, we only have twenty minutes to get you to the ceremonial arch, so let's keep moving forward."

The three finished with the yards of tulle and silks cascading from Ikram's shoulders. They bound her bodice with hundreds of baby pearls strung together by local divers and brought to the island for this occasion. Qamar placed the crown of baby's breath flowers woven with silk ribbons of the palest lavender colour on the brides head. Ikram chose to go barefoot to her wedding ceremony. Lily and Qamar wore the same style of draped dress but were sure to make it understated compared to Ikram's wedding attire.

Aglaope looked at the vision her daughter had become as a young woman. She felt this young woman was the one truth in her life that no person would ever question as goodness personified. Aglaope next looked at her mother who she spent almost an entire life being at odds with. Mel was busy with Aglaope's sisters weaving tiny flowers with clover into a delicate outer cape to cascade from Ikrams shoulders. This was woven with experienced hands. Mother taught them as small children to weave tiny flowers and grasses from the meadows into almost any garment. Aglaope remembered how easy life was for her and her sisters before that day Persephone come to visit. A gentle laugh in the room brought her back to the present.

It was Ikram laughing at just how many flowers she was wearing. She was telling Qamar and Lily that she would look like a garden and not a bride. Everyone was happy today. Aglaope saw her mother smiling at Ikram, then at her.

"Thank you, mother for the beautiful weaves," Aglaope said sincerely as she held her mother's hand.

Mel looked at her daughter and said to her, "I did not have the opportunity to help any of my daughters with a wedding and so I have looked forward very much to Ikrams wedding. Thank you, Aglaope for letting me share a part of this day. Ikram is a beautiful bride and a beautiful young woman the same as her mother." Mel squeezed her daughters hand to let her know they should take a seat for the ceremony.

A gentle breeze cooled the afternoon sun. A lonely pan flute somewhere close to the arch played a melody of love for the bride and groom. As Qamar and Lily slowly wandered to the ceremonial arch they tossed whole jasmine flowers to the ground as a soft carpet for Ikram's unclad feet. Two small island boys followed the pair, releasing brightly coloured small butterflies as they walked behind the half sisters.

Standing beside Chrys, Saon turned to see his betrothed, a true vision of loveliness. He was absolutely sure at this moment in time that he had made the right decision in having only Ikram as the one woman to share his life. Ikram held her gaze steady as she looked into Saon's eyes, unwavering until the ceremony ended. Everyone on the island let out cheers and laughter for them. Lively dancing music began. Lily watched as the men all joined hands to dance to their traditional music.

The food and celebrations would last all night. People would visit their neighbours, congratulate the bride and groom as well as their families. It was a happy time for the people living on Samothrace.

Lily boldly held the hand of Chrys as they mingled after the wedding. This was a declaration from the two of them of their intentions. They found their friends throughout the crowded festivities telling everyone they met just what their intentions would be. The couple come across the entourage from Tangier. Saon and Ikram had invited Zharah to the wedding along with a few others they met while attending parties at the hill top villa in Tangier.

Zharah congratulated them and spoke to Lily, "Lily, did I not tell you one day we would become as sisters?"

Lily responded with a light laugh. "Yes, Zharah, you did." Lily kept in mind that it was Zharah who unwittingly let the grae ladies know that she walked every evening to the yacht in the Jeddah Harbour to visit Chrys. Lily wanted to chastise Zharah but thought better of it. This was not the time or place. It may turn into even more trouble for her. She had learned that Ceto had already dealt with Zharah. Chrys was the favoured family member of Ceto. Zharah would be very careful about pleasing him and his bride to be. Zharah watched the two with a guarded expression wander toward the shores edge to be alone. As the shadows grew along with the hour, Lily noticed the giant olive and fig trees beginning to come alive, lighting up with millions of tiny fireflies. She looked over toward Chrys deep in conversation with a group from the villa in Tangier. Lily welcomed this time to herself to look over the expansive wedding venue. It was out of a fairytale. The young man playing the pan flute was as tiny as an elf or fairy. He was dressed in a grey green leotard suit. She noticed his ears were abnormally large and pointed. Just then he winked at her. Lily lowered her gaze, embarrassed for staring. She felt a hand on her shoulder and placed her hand over it thinking it was Chrys, only to realize it was a woman's soft skin. Mnemosyne laughed lightly.

"Did I frighten you, Lily? I was watching you taking in all of the different people and venues here. Yes, you are right about the fairies and elves here. Samothrace is home to water nymphs and so elves and fairies feel quite at home here. It is a peaceful island. I saw you admiring the trees lighting up with the fireflies. This has been a tradition since the dawn of time that millions of insects are lured to the trees. The children spend days placing honey all over the trees with the aid of wildflowers. This attracts the fireflies. They will feast all night long on the honey as we will on our food. I know this isn't the time for me to speak to you but please remember one thing, Lily. You are like a baby discovering a completely new world. There are a lot of differences in this world than what you have seen as you grew up in Forgotten Cove. I know Melpomene and your father have introduced you to some of our world with the layering and fast travel but when it comes to being inside a mind or reading the thoughts of others, you have barely scratched the surface."

"Oh, Mnemosyne, everyone has been so kind to my mother and me," Lily began to answer; I know I have a long way to go and a lot to learn. I have decided to apply myself to it all with much more seriousness. Sometimes I feel like such an outsider with Ikram and Qamar. They were always surrounded with this life, growing up in it." Lily hung her head, "I feel like a child."

Mnemosyne drew Lily into her arms. "Lily, you are a child in our world. Most of us have seen the crusades. Take your time; go slow with what you learn. If anything should be learned from your abduction, then it must be that you learn to become more alert. Watch the animals to learn this. Now, go to Chrys and enjoy the wedding." With that little heart to heart talk Mnemosyne gently nudged Lily back toward Chrys, turned and walked off toward the bride and groom.

28

The beautiful day and night would come to an end. Lily decided throughout the evening it would be better for her if she returned to Jeddah with Qamar and Arabella. She decided it was important for her future to learn from the residents of the villa just what was the most important for a serious half mortal to learn. Lily decided to show more responsibility with her actions. She would contact Ellie regularly concerning her mother. One part of her agenda was to travel to Olympus with Melpomene in a few weeks to meet the family of Chrys. Lily was excited but a bit frightened to meet his family. She would be escorted to the Phorcys cavern by Hermes, Calli and Mel.

It was very late in the night that Lily arrived at the villa in Jeddah. Shortly after she arrived in her sleeping quarters, she was given a note by one of the newer staff members in the villa. The note said she was to call Ellie as soon as possible, regardless of the hour.

"Mother, has something happened?" Lily spoke aloud as she dialled Ellie's house. Ellie didn't answer the telephone so Lily decided to call her mother's house to speak with the nurse in charge of her mother. It was Ellie who picked up the phone to answer her call.

An excited Ellie told Lily that Hannah had been heard several times by the nurses on duty calling out Jacks name. "Lily at least we know she can speak and remembers Jack, so she has a memory. The doctor told me this was normal with a person in a coma. He said not to read too much into it, that your mother does have a long road to recovery. I felt I had to update you. She is still unconscious but her eyes flicker a lot when she calls for Jack. She moves her hands a lot now so we know she is not paralyzed."

"Ellie, please tell me, do you think I should come home now? It might be anytime that she comes out of the coma."

Ellie responded by telling Lily that it should be her decision. Lily told Ellie that she would call her later in the morning to let her know what the decision would be on returning to Forgotten Cove. As she crossed the room to open the windows to the cool late night air, Lily thought about the last evening she spent in this room. Her life was on a different path now. Still she felt the impulse to go to Chrys tonight even though they had just parted hours before. As she was deciding on whether to go to the yacht or not to go, a slight tapping on her door broke her thought pattern. It was Qamar, asking her to join them for tea in the majlis. Traditionally guests visiting the villa were greeted in a formal sitting room called a majlis. It was separated from the living quarters of the family. This was intended for family privacy away from guests.

"This must be because we have a guest." Lily said to Qamar.

"Yes we do and at such a late hour. We have Chrysaor, along with Ceto and Phorcys," replied Qamar.

Lily was out the door of her bedroom before Qamar could finish speaking.

"Qamar, has something happened?" Lily asked, as she walked quickly toward the majlis.

"Lily, I don't know the answer to that, but mother and I will sit with you only because Hermes, Mel and the others are not here at this time. It is very strange that Ceto has left Olympus. Mother said she never leaves Olympus. Anyway, don't worry, we will stay with you," replied Qamar again.

Lily and Qamar entered the sitting room to join Arabella. Chrys moved to Lily's side to greet her. The two people with him were staring at her as she entered the room.

Chrys took her by her hand and introduced her. "Ceto, Phorcys, I want you to meet Lily, daughter of Hermes and someday to be my wife in a marriage to each other forever."

Then Chrys spoke to Lily, "Lily these two people are as close to grandparents as I could ever hope for. I would give my immortality up for them. These people are the patriarch and matriarch of my family, Phorcys and Ceto."

Ceto stared at Lily. A small smile was beginning to form on her stone-like face. Lily exhaled finally accepting it as an approval. "Lily, I had to come to the villa to meet you. Chrys has talked to us a lot about you. He is right. You do somehow resemble Melpomene. That is because you are of the Zeus lineage. But he is right too in telling me that your grey eyes with tiny green lights in them are the color eyes my daughter Medusa had while she lived. She was a beautiful girl and you also have that kind of beauty. Zharah called on us with a visit earlier this evening. She told us of her attendance at the wedding of Hermes son to Melpomenes granddaughter. Zharah said that we must see you for ourselves. She told us that seeing you dressed for the wedding made her realize just how much you resemble Medusa. She is right in saying that. I have come to Jeddah tell you that you have approval from Phorcys and I. We will speak again to you closer to the wedding. Now we must leave." With that the two abruptly left the villa with Chrys, Chrys telling Lily quickly as he left that they would talk later.

Qamar, Arabella and Lily looked at each other, speechless. Arabella was the first to speak. "What was that all about? They were here less than five minutes. I was sure that Melpomene told me that she would escort you to Olympus to meet Ceto."

Lily answered. "You are right, Arabella. Mel and my father were to take me in the next few weeks to meet Chrys's family. I was to wait for them to come here to the villa to bring me to Zeus and Mnemosyne for an introduction set up by them with their neighbours. I guess that may have changed. I am really tired from the wedding and all of the traveling lately. I think I am going to sleep the rest of tonight and half of tomorrow. I will be saying good-night to both of you right now." Lily slowly made her way up the ornate staircase, feeling every step harder to climb than the one before it.

Lily wondered what the real reason may have been for Ceto and Phorcys to come to the villa with Chrys this evening unannounced. She was sure that Mel told her she would meet them on Olympus with Hermes and her both on hand to help her answer any questions that she felt uncomfortable to answer. This was the second time Zharah had been talking to others concerning her. Lily felt tired. With so much travel in the last while, she was beginning to miss being at home in her own bed in Forgotten Cove spending a little time just wandering the beaches looking for pretty shells that attracted her. Her life had changed. Was she just feeling a little frightened at the prospect of spending a lifetime with Chrys who would be gone all the time diving for the blood red coral? Lily wanted to marry Chrys to spend time living at the villa and at home in Forgotten Cove with him. Maybe she was too much of a small town girl for Chrys. Why was she feeling this doubt? Lily guessed it was because she was tired and needed to sleep for more than a few hours. Before she could remember to return the call to Ellie, Lily dosed.

29

After a late morning telephone conversation with Ellie, Lily felt a little more encouraged that she had chosen wisely when she made her decision to return to Forgotten Cove. She felt it was a good decision to stay close to her mother at this time now that Hannah was beginning to talk aloud while still in her coma. Lily had also made another decision that she would find the boy in the wheelchair she met on the beach all those years ago. Lily discussed this with Ellie who then told her that she would return her call within the hour. It was easy enough for Lily to wait for Ellie to call her. She used the time to think over the exciting future she had with the immortals. They were her family.

Later with the few telephone calls made by Ellie, Lily was given the information that the family of the boy in the wheel chair lived less than ten miles from Forgotten Cove. They returned to the beach every year on weekends. They did this to enjoy the walks with their son Edward along the old boardwalk. Ellie told Lily the trips to the seashore in Forgotten Cove calmed Edward. The ancient boardwalk run the entirety of the beachfront up to the old wooden dock where fishing boats moored since it was built. There were a few newer boat launches in the area for recreational craft but yearly the old dock was only upgraded for the fishing boats and the boardwalk remained the attraction.

Clearly, Lily had to let Chrys know of her plans to return to Forgotten Cove. Lily next asked Arabella to have a driver take her to the dock and be prepared to wait for her. Later Chrys greeted her with a gentle hug.

"Lily, I am so sorry for just dropping back in to the villa last evening, especially after our late return from the wedding. I was surprised that Ceto and Phorcys would visit me here on the yacht. They were here when I arrived back from dropping you at the villa. Ceto told me she decided to visit Jeddah to meet you. This was decided shortly after Zharah stopped over on Olympus to tell them we had announced our betrothal at Saon and Ikrams wedding. Ceto was under the impression that it would be announced in a month by Phorcys and Zeus on behalf of their families on Olympus."

Lily was surprised at the way their betrothal was to be announced by his family. "Chrys, I hope we haven't angered the families or embarrassed them."

"That's not even a consideration you should be thinking of, Lily. Our life and our wedding announcement is our decision. Whatever makes us comfortable is exactly what we will do, but it would have been a lot more traditional if Zharah would have left it for our family to announce. Ceto and Phorcys should have been told by your family patriarch," answered Chrys.

'I am so glad you feel that way, Chrys," Lily continued, "and I am glad I met Ceto and Phorcys but I found it odd that it was such a short visit."

Chrys handed Lily a glass of lemonade filled with ice chips and mint leaves. "You will come to understand Ceto more as you get to know her. We will not be spending hardly any time at her home but you will from time to time. This is because of the grae ladies. They continue to live at home part time. We never know when they will drop in. Further, this is a very rare occurrence for Ceto to leave her home on Olympus. Whatever else Zharah told Ceto about you, she must have spiked her interest in meeting you right away. She did tell Ceto about the whispers of you sharing the unearthly beauty of Medusa. I guess Ceto was curious about this resemblance to Medusa."

They both laughed, still a little uneasy when sharing personal information. Lily began, "Oh Chrys, please don't be upset with me but so much has happened in the last five months. Everyone I meet tells me I resemble or act like someone they know. I have to become more serious with the person I am to become while I am a guest at the Zeus villa. I have not been paying attention to anything except seeing you and loving all of the attention I have been getting from others. Chrys, I come from a small fishing village on the Atlantic and very few people even notice me there. I am simply not used to this. I have to apply myself a little more in learning to be a half mortal." They laughed again. "Should I have used the term half immortal instead?" Then Chrys hugged Lily. Next he told to her to never leave him for very long at any time.

Lily caught a tear forming that was just ready to fall to her cheek. She was feeling a bit overwhelmed with what lie ahead in her life. "Chrys, I have to go to Forgotten Cove. My mother is starting to return from her coma. I have to go back and practise the disciplines of layering. Chrys, I have to become more responsible instead of playing here on your yacht like a spoiled child."

Chrys soberly replied. "You don't want to be a spoiled child like Zharah, do you Lily? I guess I knew you would become more like the daughters of Zeus. You are the daughter of Hermes. That is important to you. Lily, can I visit you?"

"Chrys, you would? I mean would you, Chrys? I would love that. It will only be a short while that I stay in Forgotten Cove," Lily bounced up and down almost childlike as she said this.

Chrys took Lily's hand in his. "Lily, I have something I had made for you before we went to the wedding on Samothrace. I didn't want to give it to you when the day was all about Ikram and Saon. I want to give it to you to wear forever, even before we marry." Chrys didn't wait for her to answer. He held Lily's wedding finger and placed the delicate silver ring with red coral stones inlaid on her finger. It was attached to a strand of the same red stones encased in the same ornate silver chain. This strand was attached to a bracelet which he fastened around Lily's wrist. Chrys looked into her eyes and said, "Lily I had this ring made with the bracelet attached so you will never lose it and it will never come off unless you take it off."

"Chrys it is so beautiful," Lily said as she gazed at the beautiful piece of jewelry. "I love the elaborate design in the silver with the beautiful garnet-coloured stones. What stone is this?"

"Lily, this is the blood red coral I dive for in the Red Sea. These stones are the red coral that formed from drops of blood that fell into the sea as Perseus flew through the night sky with the head of my ancestor, Medusa. You know that I am descendent of her." Chrys stood back to stare into Lily's eyes to see her reaction. It was as he hoped it would be. Tears splashed onto Lily's cheeks and slowly rolled down her face. She stood silent as she was searching for a response to this.

"Chrys, I will never spend a day without this on my hand. It is so precious to me." Lily hesitated, and then added, "I know what Medusa's memory means to you and to Ceto. I will cherish this forever."

the VILLA

Chrys gently held Lily in his arms until the late afternoon. He made the decision that she was the one he would share the rest of his immortal days with.

30

It was much later the same day by the time Lily had made her journey to Forgotten Cove. Ellie had already spoken with the nurses that tended Lily's mother. She had discovered that one of the night nurses went to work at the family home of the boy in the wheelchair from Lily's childhood for a few days a week to help out the family with his care. After a persuasive conversation with the nurse, Lily was told by Ellie that it would be alright for her to go with the nurse on her next visit to the family of Edward.

Ellie introduced Ashley to Lily. Lily was told again by Ashley, her mother's night nurse, that the boys name was Edward and not to be shortened to Ed or Eddy. There had been a terrible accident on the family's boat just off Chaleur Bay when he was just seven years old. Edward suffered an injury to his spinal cord and brain causing his lack of mobility. The lack of mobility was supposed to be short term. The same injury to the left side of Edwards's brain was responsible for his not speaking since that day. A few of Edward's doctors agreed that Edward did not speak or walk by choice. The grief-stricken family chose to care for him at home with the help of a live-in nanny since he was their only child. Ashley went on to tell Lily that Edward could actually stand but his mother insisted he stay in the chair. It seemed the spinal cord was not severed as originally thought. It was bruised quite badly leading up to years of Edward being unable to walk, resulting in his weakened state. Edward did not talk because he was embarrassed at the way he slurred his words. He chose to be silent. Ashley relieved the nanny a few days during the weekdays. This would help in making it easy for Lily to visit with him on those days. One thing Lily was not told was if permission were granted by Edwards's parents or the nanny for her visits. During the drive to Edwards house Ashley mentioned to Lily that she had heard her mother call out Jacks name several times. She further added that she thought her mother had also called out for Lily from deep within her coma. Ashley told Lily that she had informed Ellie of her mother actually sitting up in her sleep on one of those nights. Lily made a mental note to check with Ellie as to why she was not informed immediately of this event.

The house that came into view was an impressive old Tudor style covered in ivy. The grounds were carefully landscaped to include the rather large apple orchard. As they entered the drive Lily saw the trees, heavily laden with this year's apple crop ripening in the bright sunlight. They drove around the back of the house and entered. Ashley walked in silence ahead of her. She brought Lily into a library filled with the amazing books Edward would never read. As Lily browsed the selections, she saw that every childhood fairy tale she was read as a child lined these shelves. This gave Lily an idea. Ashley left her in the room alone, only to return in less than five minutes pushing the wheelchair. Lily could see immediately that Edward had not grown a lot from the small boy's body she saw on the beach that summer. Upon closer look she saw that his face had changed to that of a young man with his obvious need to shave.

Lily could see that he recognized her from the small twinkle in his eyes and the hint of an attempt to smile forming around his mouth. He moved his hands rapidly as if he were clapping them. Ashley shared with Lily that he wasn't very good at controlling the movement of his hands but did have a little movement whether intended or not. The nurse took her leave, telling Lily she would return in fifteen minutes. Lily moved close to him and held both of his hands in hers. Edward stared at the beautiful silver bracelet inlaid with red coral on her hand. Again he tried to clap his hands.

"Hello Edward, do you remember me from the shore long ago?" Lily began, "I know you can move your hands. No matter what anyone says, just keep trying to move them more every day."

Lily knew that Edward would be eager for her to layer him. Lily entered slowly to see the memories of the hillside she had already left with him all those years ago on the beach. At the time on the shoes edge Lily thought she was leaving him a lot of information but now today Lily saw how it was only minutes of her life she gave to him. How could she have left him with such a tiny amount of happiness? Lily felt ashamed of this and squeezed Edwards hands in hers. Her thoughts came slowly as she began with gently sitting in the opening of his unused mind.

"*Edward,*" she thought, "*I have been far away from Forgotten Cove. I flew high in the sky like the birds over the great mountains and oceans of the world. I have been to ancient cities so old; they were built hundreds of years before this country was ever discovered by man.*" He looked at her in a confused way. This all meant nothing to him. Edward had only ever been to Forgotten Cove in his lifetime, aside from being at home and to a doctor's office. Edward was still a little boy. He had not matured and would never have the benefit to grow in his mind in the same way Lily or anyone else had as they expanded their knowledge base. Lily decided perhaps Edward was a

the VILLA

lot like her; she would never grow old either. She was half immortal. Lily decided to try this again in a different way, similar to the day she met him on the beach. She could see on that day that he loved where she took him in her mind. Edward was still an infant in his life. Lily must move slower with her layering of him.

She withdrew from the layer to sit again on the sill before re-entering Edwards mind. Lily thought of how wondrous the garden at the villa in Jeddah appeared to her the first day she saw it. *Lily walked very slowly through the fragrant tangled vines of wisteria cascading down the front of the building. She reached out to caress the soft white flowers of the jasmine planted among the wisteria, inhaling the heady fragrance by cupping the flowers very close to her face, feeling the soft velvety texture of the tiny petals. Lily next walked slowly over to the area of the garden where thirty-five pairs of the thirty-nine types of the Bird of Paradise species lived. She saw a beautiful blue and black bird picking up bits of seeds from flower pods that spilled them onto the ground. The startled bird signalled the others and the sky immediately filled with a rainbow of coloured feathers as the noisy birds become airborne. The young ocelot pair brushed against her legs to say hello as they passed her on the way to laze at the gentle fountain that continuously filled the wading pool. Bees playfully moved from lotus flowers as citrus coloured frogs frightened them.* Lily slowly opened her eyes to see the boy smiling at her. He had a peaceful look in his eyes. Lily would continue these visits until his mind was filled with the natural beauty the earth offered so unselfishly of itself.

"*Edward,*" she thought, as she entered into her layer again, "*I want to show you something really beautiful. It's the fireflies lighting up the giant fig trees at my friends Ikram and Saon's wedding.*" Lily took his hands and placed them on her temples, willing him to climb inside to see her memories of the thousands of tiny blinking lights in the old fig trees. Next she gave him her memory of her cupping a tiny firefly inside of her hands, using it as a light to guide her on the darkened path. She could feel it crawling around softly. Lily heard Edward laugh aloud. She pulled back. A lone tear cascaded down his face. Lily felt the tear gently touch her own cheek as she hugged Edward. "This is what Melpomene and Mnemosyne want me to learn, Edward." she said aloud to him.

The ride home was without conversation. Ashley quickly said her good-byes and drove off toward the beachfront. Ellie was walking toward her on her way to Hannah and Lily's house. Lily waited for her before going inside the house of her mother.

"Ellie, why hasn't someone mentioned my mother actually sitting up while calling out for Jack and for me?"

Ellie paused to think before answering. "Lily, the doctors told us that sometimes people in a coma do speak and move. It does not mean that they are partially conscious or that they will have a complete memory when they come out of their coma. I decided to let it be part of the coma and continue to hope that one day your mom would open her eyes and come back to us. I did not keep it from you for any reason except I felt you had so much to deal with already. I was afraid to give you false hope since it has been many months since Hannah has been with us. I telephoned you in Jeddah just to share the bit of hope I have for her recovery."

Lily rubbed her hand up and down on Ellie's back. "I know you care so much for my mother and for me too. I have been through a lot and will go through a lot in my life but I will learn to handle everything sent my way. Now let's look in on my mother." The two went into Hannah's bedroom to get the day's update from the nurse attending her. They were told that Hannah was very restless; moving her head side to side during this nurses day shift. Lily decided she would sleep in the nurses reclining chair that night and the next few nights to be close to her mother.

Deep within her coma Hannah was watching Jack as he wandered very close to the pale grey layers. She wanted to call out to him, to tell him to take her hand and guide her so she could be with him. Mainly Hannah hesitated because she was a bit frightened. It wasn't the lighter coloured layers that frightened her. She just felt more comfortable in the darker coloured layers. Lately Hannah wanted to see just what attracted her so much in the soft black layers. She thought at times she could hear Lily crying out for her.

Lily stayed with her mom all night long and several nights after this. On the third night, at around three in the morning, Hannah sat straight up in her bed and screamed out Lily's name. Lily moved out of the chair quickly to her side. "Mom, I am here." Lily answered, grabbing hold of Hannah's hands to calm her when she began ripping the tubing away from her body.

"Oh, Lily, I was so frightened of what those hags were going to do to you. When I saw them drop you to the ground from out of that sack, I was afraid they would try to harm you." Hannah was staring around the room wide-eyed, trying to make sense of where she was. "How did we get here? Where are the others, Lily?"

Lily kept a tight grasp on her mothers flailing arms and hands. The nurse was now with them in the room telling Lily that she would call the doctor to come right away. Lily knew that her mother thought they were still on the island from where she was rescued from the grae ladies. Lily hugged her mother tightly partially to restrain her. Lily was bursting inside with the excitement of everything she would tell her mother that happened to her as she laughed aloud with great excitement much the same way she did as a small girl at a circus.

The next few days were a cause for celebration. The village soon heard that Hannah had returned. Well-wishers from Forgotten Cove come to Hannah's house to drop off homemade baking for Hannah's household. Melpomene arrived by noon the day after Hannah returned to her conscious state. Ellie soon become her old self again, chattering constantly, even to herself in an empty room. This always caused Lily to laugh at Ellie. Sounds of laughter came easy again to Hannah's house and to the people in Forgotten Cove.

By the third day of her being conscious, Hannah wanted out of bed. She was trying to be more independent than the doctor's orders wanted to allow. Ellie, Mel and Lily noticed that Hannah was not as patient as she once was. She would not take suggestions from others on her recovery time. Her explanation was that she had but one life to live and would live it how she wanted. Hannah was a very adventurous person long ago when she first arrived in Forgotten Cove, even more adventurous before she met Jack. Through the years living with him, then his dying and her raising Lily alone, Hannah had become less of a risk taker. She was almost willing to live in the shadow of Lily. The doctor advised her to take things slow for awhile but again Hannah told the doctor she would do this at the villa in Jeddah. This was a surprise to Ellie and to Mel, one not anticipated. Hannah told Lily that she would share her life more closely by staying close at her side. She did not want to sit in Forgotten Cove waiting for a visit from Lily. Lily was pleased with this. They would return together to the villa in a few weeks. Hannah informed her good friend Ellie that she would spend the summers in Forgotten Cove and the winters in Jeddah at the villa. Mel was beaming at this news.

"Hannah, it seems Ellie and I have our old friend back. I am pleased you will stay at the villa. I am sure Arabella will be very happy with this news. Ellie, you can come to visit the villa too, whenever you would like." Mel sipped her tea with a smile on her face.

Ellie answered this, "I still think Hannah should be here but I will not stand in her way to be with Lily at the villa." Then to

Hannah, "You need a period of time to recover, Hannah. Do this for Lily and for Jacks memory."

Hannah stared quizzically at Ellie before she answered and asked the question, "Who is Jack?"

With a shake of her head warning Ellie and Lily not to question Hannah's memory loss, Mel answered her back with, "Lily wants to be close to Chrys. I'm sure he misses her very much. It is a good opportunity for Hannah to get to know her daughter's husband to be." Mel held Lily's hand as she said this.

Hannah spoke next. "Lily, you and I will sit with Chrys and his family. I am not going to be left out of my daughter's life. I know Hermes wanted to accompany Lily to Chrys's family on Olympus but Lily is my daughter too, so I will meet them too."

The room was silent but only for a moment. The four women laughed and agreed on this decision. Later there was a long discussion about Hannah not having memory of Jack. They were told by the doctor that it was very common in people returning from a coma to lose bits of their memory. Mel knew better of that. Mnemosyne had recently taken Jack from Hannah's memory although it was temporary to enable her to want to return from her coma. Mnemosyne directed Hannah toward the dark she must face in her coma in order to return to the layer of the living. Hannah would be given back the memory of Jack later in her life.

31

Lily returned to the bluffs everyday for the next few weeks. She was considering how involved she should become in Edward's life. Now that she learned he could possibly speak and walk one day she had hope that her encouragement would play a role in his recovery. Lily would discuss this with Mel. Perhaps Edward's parents could be persuaded to send Edward to the villa for a short stay. In her heart, Lily wanted Chrys to be up there at the top of the bluff waiting for her whenever she made the climb up the bluffs. She sat staring across the waters in his direction so many days. Mostly she wanted to be alone to think. The bluffs above Forgotten Cove provided Lily with the familiarity of all she had ever known as a child growing up here. Her life had been uncomplicated. It was becoming very clear to her the villa was her future but still she needed the solace she found in these bluffs to indulge in the memories of the simple life she once had here.

Lily was so pleased that her mother would return to the villa with her. That meant a lot to have someone who understood her well. The recent times Melpomene had come to sit with her on the bluffs,

the VILLA

Lily could feel just how much she cared for her. Mel was happy with her progress in layering. Lily rambled on to Mel, who loved hearing of her visits to Edward. The summer was coming to an end. That evening the August moon, huge and orange was close enough to reach out and touch. It was this moon that awakened the desire to travel the world in Lily. Lily knew her future would see many of these moons with Chrys. Later the same night in front of that August moon Lily dared to fast travel alone for the first time the very great distance to the yacht. She convinced herself to be brave and off she went. It seemed only minutes later she was on the deck of the Garnet in the Jeddah harbor. When she alit Chrys spun around to see who his visitor could be. In his eyes Lily saw her future. She could see his love for her and knew this was where she belonged. He reinforced to her again they should never be apart. Chrys would return with Lily to Forgotten Cove. The two arrived at sunrise in the early morning hours as the house was coming awake.

Mel greeted the pair as they entered the house. She decided this was her opportunity and would be the right time to ask Chrys about the visit to the villa by Ceto and Phorcys. Chrys explained to Mel that the grae ladies had returned to Olympus to report to Ceto of the girl they had kidnapped. The girl was Lily. The grae ladies told Ceto that this girl looked like their sibling, her dead daughter Medusa. To them it was exciting. Ceto didn't seem to show any curiosity to the grae ladies about the girl but Medusa's gorgon sisters might be interested. The ladies decided take the kidnapped Lily to Medusa's sisters on the island to show them just how much she resembled Medusa. Ceto only become more interested herself when later Zharah went to her with the same tale of the girl Lily, who resembled Medusa so much. Ceto wanted to see this for herself, so decided to go immediately to the Zeus Villa after being told.

Mel weighed these words before responding. "That was the reason why Ceto left Olympus. Yes, you are right about the resemblance. I could see this too but kept it to myself for fear of others telling me that I am seeing what I want to see. Chrys, do you see this yourself?"

"Oh yes Mel, I see it. I have only looked at artists paintings of Medusa at Ceto's home while growing up. I think that is what attracted me to Lily in the beginning. Then as I began to know her better, I realized she had her own personality with the same kindly character I was told that Medusa had. I felt I must guard her from anyone who would intend harm toward her in our immortal world."

While this conversation was taking place, Lily brought her mother into the room. "Mother you can get to know Chrys better while Mel and I prepare a large breakfast. Come help me Mel." Lily took Mel's hand and they walked arm in arm to the kitchen.

Hannah looked at the handsome young man before her. He was not nervous at all in meeting her the second time. Chrys spoke first, "Hannah, I know you are aware that I do intend to marry your only child, Lily. I will give her everything she needs forever in her life. I will also care for you as her mother wherever you are. Nothing will ever happen to you or her by the hands of an immortal being."

"Chrys, both of you have my blessing. I can see in your eyes that what you say is true. I know you speak from your heart." Hannah hugged Chrys as Mel walked into the room carrying hot coffee for both of them.

Hannah and Lily began their preparations daily for the new life they would begin this month. Hannah developed a renewed interest in Mel and her immortal family. She could hardly wait to talk with Mel again at the villa. She was excited to spend time with Arabella too. They had already spent more than one evening in conversation about Arabella's life with the children of Zeus. It seemed Ellie was fussing over her a lot lately telling her how worried she was with

Hannah taking such a long flight. Hannah reassured Ellie that everything was fine with her health after waking from the coma and to please try to refrain from treating her as an invalid. They laughed at this.

It was weeks later, aboard Saudia Airlines, Hannah smiled at Ellie's heartfelt attempts to protect her. Ellie would never know all Hannah had been through since meeting Melpomene. Hannah decided to view her coma as a long sleep. She felt very much ready to experience life again. Hannah smiled again to herself as she thought of the past few weeks. She had found several old books at Ellie's shop. They were myths, stories of the gods. Hannah could not put them down. Some she read through more than once. It was exciting to know that she was now included in their lives. Arabella could tell her much more than the books would ever tell her. Arabella was a member of the family that stayed in the house of the family of Zeus for centuries. With these thoughts Hannah dosed off into a restful sleep for a while. She was relaxed and refreshed, eager to begin her new life.

High on Olympus in the cavern of Mnemosyne and Zeus, Mel and Calli were deep in conversation when Hermes entered. They were discussing the note left on the gate to the underworld several months ago. Hermes joined the conversation by asking Calli about her visit to Ceto to discuss the note. Zeus had instructed Calli to be his emissary for any issues that may arise among the families living on Olympus.

"Yes Hermes," started Calli, "I did go to pay a visit to Ceto and Phorcys. They did say they would investigate the notes left on the doors to the underworld in several different places. There were several of the gates with notes warning us of the danger our new half mortals faced. It seems that Euryale and Stheno had decided that the island was quite empty with more than a hundred stone souls being taken from it to give to Persephone in trade for Jack Galleghar's soul. I also decided to pay a visit to Persephone to let her know how the Phorcides and Zeus family felt about her greed. I decided to tell her how unwelcome she would be on Olympus and in Jeddah at the villa because of these souls. She obviously did take it to heart and did return more than half of the souls to the island of the Gorgons. The grae ladies decided around this time to stir up a bit of intrigue. That is when they decided to follow our new half mortals. This is the time period when they discovered what a great likeness Lily was for their sister, Medusa. They thought that they would gain great favors from Euryale and Stheno by bringing them such a prize."

Calli hesitated for a moment to sip her tea. Hermes began, "This means we still have to keep a close watch on the new half mortals. Euryale and Stheno have not seen Lily yet. Just what would they do if they saw someone with such a likeness to their sister?"

Mel interrupted, "Hermes, are you suggesting that they would hold Lily captive just because she looks like Medusa?"

Calli answered this. "No, they sure wouldn't. Ceto and Phorcys would never condone this action. I wanted to tell you what has further come from what the grae ladies caused by abducting Lily. Someone did tell the grae ladies about Lily possibly marrying Chrys. This was Zharah. It seems that she happened upon a visit to the yacht, the Garnet, belonging to Chrys, by our three new half mortals. Saon brought the three to meet Chrys very shortly after their arrival at the villa. I think it was a week after their arrival. It seems that Zharah had arrived close to the same time they were arriving and saw Lily. She told the grae ladies, who began to watch Lily when she coming to and leaving the yacht nightly. This is when they decided to take her. Zharah has been severely reprimanded by Ceto for her part in causing this to happen. Zharah knew that the grae ladies could be persuaded to do anything, so she convinced them to abduct Lily. Ceto assures me it will never happen again. Ceto also told me not to worry about the notes on the gates to the underworld. She and Phorcys will take charge of the situation in their family. Although, in saying all I have told you, I will warn you to be vigilant in dealing with Zharah. I think she may have wanted Chrys for her own husband. Lily just may be in her way."

Both Mel and Hermes nodded in agreement. They would keep Lily under close watch beginning now and forever more.

32

The villa in Jeddah appeared to have every light in the main area turned on inside and outside. Arabella had feelings a part of her own family had finally come home. She had instructed the cooks to prepare a feast for the arrival of Lily and Hannah. Arabella knew the pair may sleep for a few more hours before coming down to the enormous dining area. She next prepared extra table settings for Mel and Hermes who had arrived shortly after Hannah and Lily in the late afternoon. The table would be laden with dishes that tasted as beautiful as they appeared on the delicate china she would use for hosting special occasions. Arabella prepared her own favourite rice dish filled with nutmegs and dried limes for her guests.

Qamar was busy fussing with her long black hair, weaving gold cord through it. She applied the purple eye shadow that made her eyes even more exotic. Qamar dressed carefully in her favourite lavender and gold robes. She was so excited to see her half sister, especially since she had not seen Lily since the return from Saon and Ikram's wedding. They had so much to talk about, so many new secrets to share. Qamar had learned from Mel that Chrys gave Lily an ornate silver bracelet with the ring attached for a betrothal gift. It was silver inlaid with the red garnet coloured coral from the Red Sea that Chrys harvested. Qamar had heard from her mother long ago the coral was reported to be the drops of blood from his ancestor Medusa. Qamar thought how frightened she would be to wear such a bracelet. Voices were talking animatedly from the dining area. Qamar wandered into that part of the villa to greet her family.

Everyone at the table was so animated; they were all talking at the same time. So much had happened in the last few months. Hannah brought everyone up to date with the current state of her health and her new intentions. During the conversation Hannah asked Arabella if it was alright for her to become part of the staff and earn her keep instead of just staying at the villa as a guest. Arabella laughed at this by telling her she was welcome to help out at the enormous mansion. This would never be as a staff member of the house. Hannah was the mother of one of the descendants of Zeus so could entertain herself however she chose.

Lily laughed with abandon as she told the dinner table of layering Edward. She promised that Edward would become a major part of her life. Hermes told her it was good news that she was taking her obligation to become expert in the layering others seriously. Lily shared her betrothal gift from Chrys. She lowered her gaze as she told them of his proposal to her. The whole group admired the beautiful bracelet Chrys gave her as an engagement gift. On Lily's tiny hands the silver and red coral piece of jewellery looked magnificent as if seemed to come alive. The silver sparkled as it reflected the light from the huge chandeliers in the dining area. The red coral appeared fluid with the light dancing off of it.

Mel and Hermes took turns speaking to everyone bringing everyone up to date on the happenings at the top of Olympus. They informed everyone at the dining table of Calli's visits to Ceto and Phorcys cavern. Hermes stared into Hannah's eyes when he told them that everyone at the dinner table would escort him to Ceto and Phorcys cavern as the official visit from the house of Zeus to announce the betrothal of Lily to Chrys. Calli and an entourage from the Zeus cavern would join them when they reached Olympus.

Arabella had news to share with everyone too. She announced that she had invited Zharah to spend the next week at the villa to get to know the family better since Lily would marry her family member, Chrys. Arabella did not notice the dark look that passed between Hermes and Melpomene. No one noticed the discomfort Qamar was now beginning to feel at this announcement.

Shortly after a long meal Lily and Qamar went outside to sit in the garden. Lily looked at Qamar who was busy playfully teasing the ocelots. "Qamar, you know you can't hide anything from me. You have been avoiding looking at me all evening. What is wrong? Have I said or done something to offend you?"

"Oh, Lily, I am so glad you noticed. I have wanted to have this conversation for so long. Do you remember when we began going to the yacht every night? I didn't feel right in stealing past the guards to the villa at night. I always had an uncomfortable feeling that we were being watched by someone. Now I know that it wasn't imagined. We were being watched by someone from the villa and at the same time by the grae ladies. After the first time Chrys took us to Tangier it began to be even more uncomfortable for me. I dreaded going to the yacht. I felt very uncomfortable when I noticed the group of hooded people watching us on so many occasions. I never told anyone but I heard Zharah tell them which one of us was Lily. Lily, I am so sorry. I feel like it was my fault you were abducted. After the abduction it was much too late to say anything to anyone about how uncomfortable I felt. Then when your mother had the accident…" Qamar hesitated, hanging her head, instead of finishing the sentence.

Lily was startled. "Qamar, please stop, I don't blame you. The grae ladies would have found an opportunity sooner or later even if you had tried to warn me. I gave them the opportunity by going out alone to see Chrys, so it is my own fault and not yours."

"Lily, I feel really uncomfortable too that my mother invited Zharah to stay here at the villa for a week," Qamar almost whispered. "I knew this a few days ago and never spoke up to her, to tell her that Zharah was trouble for us. I know that is selfish and the visit is not about me but I can't help my feelings."

Lily smiled, "Well then, Qamar, you will have to help me to make Zharah feel the same level of discomfort you feel so she won't want to stay here at the villa. I feel the same way about her. Mel told me it was Zharah who practically set me up for my abduction. I think she wants Chrys for herself."

The two laughed. Qamar spoke first. "It's great that we feel the same about her. Lily, I have been learning the art of secret layering. We could use it to layer Zharah and make her feel she doesn't want to be here."

"Qamar, you wouldn't dare. What is that, this secret layer?"

"Well," Qamar started, "it starts when you stealthily sneak up on someone when they are in a contemplative state. They are not aware that you are looking for a sill, so you can enter them without them even knowing. I have tried it on the ocelots and used it once on my mother. I made the ocelots run all over looking for who was watching them. I made my mother believe her long dead ancestors were here trying to contact her. I heard her asking in every room she was cleaning if Hayghar was here with her."

Lily laughed aloud. "Then this is how we will make Zharah leave. Both of us will layer her at once, secretly. Agreed?"

Qamar nodded and the two girls giggled as they hugged.

33

Lily and Qamar failed several times while attempting to secretly layer Zharah during the week she was visiting. Zharah finally confronted Lily with it.

"Lily, you and Qamar are not a match for me. You should know this by now and remember it forever. I have lived many years longer than you ever will. I have a lot of experience that comes with those years I have been on earth. This means I am smart enough to not interfere with Chrys's intentions with you. I am sure he will tire of you soon enough anyway. Your little half sister, Qamar and you do not seem want me here at the villa. I will leave but you would do well to know who you are dealing with the next time you visit Tangier with Chrys."

"Ceto and Phorcys will keep you under control, Zharah. Any business between Chrys and I is not your business. I can be civil with you for Chrys but I will keep the distance needed to protect myself from you," finished Lily as she left the room.

Hours later Qamar come to Lily's sitting room to tell her that Zharah did leave the villa with a message to all that they should know who they are dealing with. Qamar related to Lily that her mother had been told by Aglaope several times that Zharah was the most powerful witch in Tangier. They decided to keep their efforts this last week to themselves. If Mel or Hermes knew what they were attempting to do it may anger them. It was time to get on with learning advanced techniques to enhance their ability to fast travel. Both of the girls felt silly for failing at the attempts to secretly layer Zharah to make her feel uncomfortable enough to leave but were relieved when she finally did leave.

It was hours later after Zharah left the villa that she stood on her terrace in Tangier and stared at the movement in the waves. A few of them were white capping due to an eager wind that also cooled the terrace of her villa. On this evening she was feeling a sense of great satisfaction with her new acquisition. She was unsure of how she was going to use the blood red coral she had secretly taken from Lily's bracelet. Ever since Zharah was a young girl she listened to the stories about the precious red coral from the elder immortals. The immortals that visited the cavern where she grew into a young woman were mostly family in one way or another way. Zharah prided herself in being descendent of one the Hesperides and Atlas. Her family patriarch had fled Olympus using the cover of a dark night. Atlas decided to live in the garden of the Hesperides located close to modern day Tangier. She had only ever knew Tangier as home, first in the cavern hidden deep in the Atlas Mountains and for the last century in this aging villa that she had come to love so much.

Zharah spent much of her childhood learning ancient magic, magic that could turn a human to stone on the outside. She learned this technique from Ladon, the serpent man that guarded her family in the garden. Ladon was a descendant of Ceto and Phorcys son, the first Ladon. Zharah had dreamed since she was a child to marry into the family of Ceto and Phorcys but she would come to experience great rejection from Ladon as she grew into the beautiful young woman she would become in her immortality.

Now, centuries later after Ladon rejected her, it appeared that Chrys, who was also a descendent of Medusa, was going to reject her by marrying Lily. Zharah had to find a way to become a vital part of the family who so cruelly rejected her. The small piece of blood red coral may be her answer. In Zharah's mind she was looking for any small part of Medusa such as DNA that may be left hidden in the coral she had taken from Lily's bracelet. The DNA would be the precious life code of Medusa. If Zharah could not marry a Phorcyde then she decided she would have the DNA replicated somehow. Right now she really had no idea how she would do this but she would find a way, no matter the cost. Zharah had an idea, a crazy idea forming in her mind to go to England or Germany to find someone to help her with research. She had heard about test tube children. Her mind raced as she thought of the great favors she would receive if somehow she could be implanted with a child. Ceto would kneel at her feet if she knew Zharah was carrying Medusa and could bring her precious daughter back into the world. Zharah was feeling hope for her future as she carefully planned her visit to the research centre in Germany.

34

Lily had a wedding to begin planning for in her future. She had to decide where it would take place. Did she dare to plan it to take place in Forgotten Cove? It would please Ellie and her mother if she decided to wear her mothers dress. How would Chrys feel about this? It may be better to have the wedding on Olympus. The area was remote and secretive with the families that resided in the caverns. They may not appreciate the publicity it would bring to the mountain. These decisions kept her busy. Lily found that she had gained a lot of confidence with the fast travel. Several times in the past week she had visited Samothrace with Chrys. Lately he did not show interest to visit Zharah in Tangier. Lily was relieved.

Hannah was very happy these days with her new role in the family of Zeus. Becoming a mother of the bride was something Hannah thought she would not have to consider for a few more years. There would be a lot of wedding shopping that Arabella would assist her with. Hannah received a note from Aglaope expressing to Hannah that she too would be happy to assist Hannah with the plans for her daughters wedding. Hannah was unsure how she felt being friendly toward Aglaope. Aglaope treated her like a sibling but Hannah felt something was not right between them yet. Hermes seemed to be paying a lot of attention to her lately. Hannah was unsure that she wanted Hermes attention. It was flattering but at the same time embarrassing to her when Arabella was present.

Life had indeed changed for Hannah. It wasn't the life she had ever expected when she left New York. She remembered one summer long ago she left with intention to drive up the coast of the Atlantic as far as Chaleur Bay. Bits of her memory of Jack were returning to her. Forgotten Cove was where she had Lily, her reason for great joy in this world. She certainly never thought that people like Melpomene and her family even existed. Mel had come into her life and showed her a different world, a world hidden in the layers that make up the very fabric of our lives. Hannah had a rough childhood with her mother being a drug user. Hannah remembered really not caring when she was alone because her mother had not returned home for days at a time. Despite this, Hannah finished her nursing degree and enjoyed a great professional career. Meeting Mel satisfied her craving for adventure, although some of the adventures were not what she would have chosen to partake in. Hannah sat in the garden late this night enjoying the cool air. Mel surprised her with a visit and began a conversation that confirmed again to Hannah, Mel knew her every thought.

"Hannah, my friend, we have been through a lot in the past years since I met you on the shore in Forgotten Cove. You have joined our family and raised a daughter of Zeus for us. I know at times you thought our family was quite strange, especially toward the beginning of our friendship. A little more must make sense to you with everything we have been through together. I am sure it was your destiny to mother a half mortal child of Hermes."

"Oh Mel, so much has happened. Lily has informed me that the wedding should be a least a year from now to give her a chance to study the ways of being a half mortal. She still has a lot more she must learn from you. I am hoping she will come to meet all of your sisters and daughters. I would like that for myself too, Mel. I am beginning to really feel at home at the villa with Arabella and her family," finished Hannah.

"Well then, Hannah lets start right away. We will discuss Lily. Lily has learned the basics of layering and fast travel. Her education as a half mortal doesn't stop there. We have noticed a bit of rivalry between Lily and Zharah. Ordinarily there will be some rivalry between young women when they both have an interest in the same young man. Even though Chrys has decided he wants to marry Lily, a person such as Zharah will not stand by and let the wedding just move forward. Zharah is an immortal with strong ties to the underworld. She practices an ancient form of witchcraft taught to her by the sisters of Medusa and by Ladon. Ladon is a serpent man who guards an ancient garden of her ancestors. He is named for the long dead Ladon and obviously uses his own magic to benefit himself. This magic lets the user turn those they choose into a stone-like statue. The person can't move from the moment the spell is cast upon them. They usually die a frightening death with not being able to escape from this state. Somehow the original Ladon escaped death by other immortals to produce many children by the Hespirides. His descendant, also named Ladon, passed the stone spell down through the ages. Zharah is capable of using it. I am not telling you of her power to frighten you, Hannah. Zharah knows very well what would happen to her by Chrys's hand if she ever attempted to harm Lily."

"Mel," Hannah interrupted, "Lily and I just had a conversation about this less than an hour ago. It seems that Arabella has already warned Qamar about Zharah's capabilities. Zharah has been called the "Witch of Tangier" by the people living in that area. If this is all true then we must guard the girls."

"Yes she is called by this title," continued Mel, "I think Zharah loves the attention. Our biggest concern here at the villa is to complete some of Lily's training. She needs to learn to quickly read a mind and take control of every situation she finds herself in. Our world is filled with those who play at harming another immortal or half mortal. Among the older immortals, we know we are too strong to suffer from any spell such as Demeter cast on my daughters. Lily, being so young would be very vulnerable to a situation such as that. You see my daughters had not been taught to defend themselves when Demeter decided their fate and so they were easily changed into sirens. My girl's father and I had to stand by helpless when it all happened."

Hannah interrupted Mel, "Mel if you were so powerful at the time then why did you not have the spell reversed?"

"It's just not that easy. We cannot undo what another has cast. It is sad but the immortal who is casting the spell can't undo their spells either. It has to be approached from another angle to relieve the damage and that is all we can do. As you have been told Lily is half mortal and therefore can't cast spells but she can learn to defend herself. That is what she will learn in the next few months. Meanwhile we will keep a close watch on the residents of this villa," finished Mel.

"I am ready for all of this," said Hannah. "I want to learn everything I need to stay in Lily's life. Do you have time to teach me, Mel?"

"Hannah lets begin. We will talk through the night the way we did all those years ago. Let's get moving on with the world I promised to show you. Do you remember all those years ago I told you I have a world to share with you?" Hannah nodded assent. Mel continued, "Tonight Hannah you will learn everything you want to know about my sisters."

From the very comfortable overstuffed chair where she sat, Hannah smiled at Melpomene as she opened the bottle of rare wine Hermes left for them to share on an evening such as this. This was a new beginning for Hannah and her daughter Lily, one she was eagerly anticipating. She reached for the wine, smiling, seeing her reflection in the half filled glass, wondering just where life among the muse sisters would take her next.

After seven months passed, in another villa, worlds away from the Zeus villa, the powerful witch watched the lightning storm. She caused it to strike over and over again as people ran for safety. Zharah laughed a bitter laugh. Words were still stinging her. The young research scientists laughed when she asked them to look for DNA in her piece of blood red coral. Next she told them her plan to extract the DNA to use for a test tube baby. Two of them left the room, taking offence at this proposal, feeling she was treating them as fools. The remaining scientist told her that coral is not solidified blood and so could not possess human DNA and the meeting abruptly ended. Zharah hastily retreated, returning to her villa high above the shoreline in Tangier.

Tonight she enjoyed her lightning storm, scattering people in every direction. With her anger at the scientists finally well vented, Zharah opened the terrace doors and entered. She wanted to see her latest acquisition. A full seven months had passed since she obtained the valuable prize. Zharah stared at the handsome but rather terrified young man and smiled, "Hello Edward".

About the Author

Maureen Bukhari grew up on the Great Lakes surrounded by a large family. She has been creating stories since she was 12 years old, helping people to see the world through eyes that open just a bit wider to the possibilities around them.

While the wheels of her imagination have never stopped spinning, she spent much of her professional career as a medical laboratory technologist, working and traveling in the Middle East and Europe, where she visited the ancient antiquities of the world—and found inspiration in their far-reaching shadows.

Maureen now lives in Calgary with her husband and the two cats that run their house. A self-proclaimed dreamer, she spends her days writing, gardening, and volunteering at the family travel agency.

You can visit her at www.maureenburtonbukhari.com to find her social media sites.